HONEY OF A HURRICANE

∎

Maile Spencer Honolulu Tour Guide Mysteries

∎

Kay Hadashi

Honey of a Hurricane

Honey of a Hurricane
Maile Spencer Honolulu Tour Guide Mysteries
Kay Hadashi. Copyright 2020. © All Rights Reserved.
Revised content, July 2021.
Cover art by author adapted from Kingwood Creations.

ISBN: 9798696546346

This is a work of fiction. Characters, names, places, dialogues, and incidences are used factiously or products of imagination. Any resemblance to actual persons, businesses, events, or locales, unless otherwise denoted as real, is purely incidental. No part of any character should be considered real or reflective of any real person, living or dead. Information related to current events should be considered common knowledge and can easily be found in real life.

www.kayhadashi.com

Honey of a Hurricane

Chapter One

Maile was sick and tired of being woken every morning by her neighbors across the hall. She thought their fighting had come to an end the week before when they kissed and made up, but it was starting all over again. Peeking out the little peephole in her door, the Mendozas at least were keeping it inside their apartment this morning. When she heard something break, maybe a lamp thrown in the heat of the moment, she wrapped her bed sheet around her like a toga and went across the hall to complain.

Just as she was about to bang her fist on their door, she heard noises that weren't exactly fighting. Pressing her ear against the door for a moment, she discovered an entirely different manner of passion was being waged between husband and wife right then, rather than their usual morning spat. Tiptoeing, she went back to her apartment.

That's when she found her door had swung closed and she was locked out.

Maile continued to rattle her doorknob trying to get into her own place, while loving passion raged between the neighbors on the other side of the door behind her.

"Come on…" Maile muttered, while listening to the wife call out in her native language. Of all the times she was glad she didn't understand Filipino languages, this time was the most important. She gave her door one last shove before quitting.

Her neighbor Rosamie had a spare key for Maile's door, but she was indisposed right then, and from the sounds of it, it would be a while before she was available. She wasn't going to stand around in the hallway listening to them while dressed as an ancient Greek toga model. All she could do was go downstairs to the landlady's apartment and asked to be let in.

Mrs. Taniguchi was already dressed and had her thin silver hair pinned to her head when she answered the door. The security chain was still across when the door opened. She blinked once when she saw Maile standing there, wrapped in the sheet. "New dress?"

Maile tried smiling but failed. "Got locked out of my room. Mind letting me back in?"

"No more keys?"

"My keys are inside and I'm outside, and there's a locked door between us."

"Want to get in your room?" the old lady asked.

"That's the idea." When a biker dude came down the hall dressed in leathers and boots headed to his room, Maile attempted to achieve a higher level of modesty with her toga. "The sooner, the better."

"Wait," Mrs. Taniguchi said, closing the door. Maile listened to the TV being turned down and a few dishes clattering in the sink. When she heard the toilet flush, she figured she'd been forgotten and knocked on the door again. The landlady opened the door right away with a cross look to her face. "Is there a hurry?"

Maile followed the lady to the stairs that led up. "Standing around wrapped in a sheet, so yeah, I might be in a hurry."

"Why only wearing a sheet? Young lady like you should know better than to go out in a sheet."

"I didn't go out. I only went across the hall to complain about the noise."

"You went out dressed like that to visit the Mendozas?" By then, they were at Maile's door, and Mrs. Taniguchi was going through the laborious process of trying one key after another in the lock. From the sounds of it, the Mendozas were still in the process of unlocking their labor of love. When something fell to the floor with a loud clunk, Mrs. Taniguchi stopped working with the keys and looked Maile up and down. "You should've taken your keys."

Maile tried covering more of herself with the sheet. "It's not like that."

The landlady finally got the door open. She remained in the doorway so Maile couldn't close it.

"I understand. I was lonely too, when my husband left me. But a young lady needs to be discreet."

"I didn't…I wasn't…it's not like that, I said."

"You'll find someone. In fact, I have a nephew. Maybe not so bright, doesn't have much to talk about, but he's a good boy. If you like…"

Maile tried sweeping her landlady out of the room with the door. By then, the flow of passions had ebbed across the hall. "I'm sure he's nice."

"I'll invite him for Sunday dinner."

"I think I'm busy." Maile finally got Mrs. Taniguchi's feet pushed back out of the way and the door closed. She barely had all the locks and deadbolts thrown when there was a knock.

Maile looked at the door with her hands on her hips, but didn't open it. "Thank you, Mrs. Taniguchi! I owe you a favor!"

There was another knock, this one more insistent. She peeked through the peephole, expecting to see an angry landlady, ready to hand out a lecture about how nice the building used to be, and how she wished she could get retirees as tenants, instead of people who caused so much trouble. Instead, it was Rosamie, her neighbor, with disheveled hair and a broad smile on her face.

Maile unlocked everything. "Hi. What's up?"

"Was that you in the hall a minute ago?"

"Yeah, I locked myself out and Mrs. Taniguchi had to let me in."

"Why didn't you knock? I have your key," Rosamie said. She pushed her way into Maile's room.

"It sounded like…I wasn't sure if you were up yet."

"Oh, yeah, we were…" Rosamie looked over her shoulder at her own door still hanging open. "…you know, busy."

"It sounded like it." If Maile was going to be up, she might as well get some gossip out of her neighbor. She put a kettle of water on the stove to boil. "Tea?"

"I should get breakfast started. Kinda hungry."

"I should think so. I bet the kids are."

"Oh, the kids are at their uncle's place for the weekend."

"That's convenient. You can sleep in for a change."

"Yes, sleep in." After looking over her shoulder again, Rosamie closed the door. "Maile, I have a brother-in-law…"

"I'm sure he and his family are nice."

"No, he's single. I was thinking…"

Maile got the door open and steered Rosamie toward it. "He sounds great. Say hi to him for me."

"Maybe you could come over for dinner on Sunday?"

"Oh, what a shame! I just promised to spend Sunday with Mrs. Taniguchi's nephew. Maybe another time."

The teakettle was whistling when Maile got back to it. Pouring water over her tea bag in her mug, she wondered what there was for breakfast. She didn't have to go through cabinets to know they were nearly empty.

"Nobody wants to take me to breakfast?" She sat at her table and sipped. "Breakfast I could do. Nothing particularly romantic about breakfast."

She didn't like sugar in her tea, but she put three packets in her mug anyway.

"Doesn't have to be a single guy. Doesn't even have to be a guy. Just a plate of eggs. Hash browns would be good. And bacon. Coffee with cream. Now, if Mrs. Taniguchi's sleepy nephew showed up right now and invited me to breakfast, I think I'd take him up on it."

She sipped her tea for a moment.

"I wonder what he looks like?"

Maile sipped again.

"Who cares what he looks like? Apparently, he doesn't talk much, so I wouldn't have to hear about the great bargain he got on his truck ten years ago."

She added another packet of sugar.

"Probably a redneck bean farmer in Waimanalo."

She finished her tea and poured another mug of water.

"Waimanalo would be an okay place to live. I wonder what bean farmers eat for breakfast? Raise some chickens for fresh eggs. Grow potatoes for hash browns. Raise a pig for…no, trade eggs for bacon."

Maile was still draped in her sheet when there was another knock at the door. She set down her mug and straightened her toga.

"My Waimanalo prince has arrived," she whispered, going to the door. She looked out the peephole to see who it was. "Oh, him."

She rewrapped in the sheet and tied a tighter knot before unlocking the door and looking out the gap the security chain allowed. Two people were there, a male acquaintance and a female stranger. She looked back and forth between them.

"David, what brings you to the Coconut Palms Land of Luxury so early in the morning?"

"You do, Ms. Spencer."

"Me? I haven't done anything lawyers would find interesting. In fact, I was feeling a little lonely without a courtroom to pointlessly sit in for hours on end."

David Melendez, a lawyer that Maile had met recently, flashed a courtroom smile. "We're not here about a court case. May we come in?"

Maile looked back and forth between the two of them again. If Honolulu's most expensive lawyer looked uneasy, the woman with him looked downright uptight. She'd learned enough about lawyers and federal agents to know that wasn't a good situation. "About?"

"Something that shouldn't be discussed in the hallway," the woman said.

"If it's about Prince Aziz, that Circuit Court District Attorney from the federal government has promised me that I was no longer involved in his case."

David and the woman with him shared glances. "It's not about him."

"What's it about, then?" she asked.

"About you making some money in trade for a few hours of your time."

"I don't do special tours," she said easing the door closed. "You'll have to book through Manoa Tours."

Melendez got his toe inside the door. "Not a tour."

She tried pressing the door into his foot. "Still not interested."

"It's legit."

"I'm sure it is," she said as she put her shoulder against the door.

"Cash."

She let the pressure off the door. "When?"

"Soon. Only a few hours of easy duty, and paid in full at the end," the woman said.

Maile took off the security chain and eased the door open slightly. She used one foot to block the door and kept a hand on it and the doorjamb, in case she needed to slam the door closed. "Doing what? Because I already have a job."

"Yes, I heard from Lopaka you're back at Manoa Tours. Good for you. Would you like to make a little extra on the weekend?" David asked.

"When did you talk to Lopaka?"

"Yesterday afternoon. We went to the Manoa Tours office looking for you, but you'd left by then. Lopaka is your tour driver, right?"

"Usually. Why?"

"He made it sound like you might be interested in lending me a hand," the woman said.

That didn't sound like Lopaka at all, but she knew David well enough that he was above trying to trick her. Something didn't smell right about the set up, and it wasn't Rosamie's burnt pancakes from across the hall. "I don't give private tours."

"Like I said, it's legit business. Mostly."

"Mostly?" Maile began shoving the door closed. "I've heard that before, and got into trouble because of it. Thanks, but no thanks."

David pushed the door open again before it could latch. "It would pay well."

"How well?"

"Depends on the outcome," the woman said.

Maile had a look at the woman. She was a cop of some sort, with pinned up blond hair, a loose blouse, dark trousers, and a jacket that likely hid a giant pistol. It was the hard look to her face that unnerved Maile the most. "Who's she?"

"Let us in so we can talk," David said.

Maile looked back at her room. The Murphy bed was unmade and still folded down, a pile of dirty laundry waited for a trip to the laundromat, while another stack waited to be folded and put away. It wasn't like she owned much, but what she had seemed messy right then. Not that money could fix any of that, but her checkbook was in a bigger mess than everything else.

Without making the bed, she folded it up into the wall and latched the door to hide it. She tightened the knot of her toga again and opened the door for them.

Chapter Two

"Would you like tea?" she asked, even before introductions were made.

"I'm fine," David said.

"If you haven't had breakfast, I was wondering if we could take you someplace?" the woman offered.

"Breakfast?" Maile turned off the burner beneath a new kettle of water. "Not yet."

"You can't go dressed like that," David said.

"I suppose not, but I can't change my clothes with the two of you in here."

The woman muttered something about changing in the other room.

"There is no other room," Maile said.

After reaching behind her back like it was a reflex, the blonde nodded at the door where the bed was hidden in the wall. "What's in there?"

"Don't ask," David said. "Maybe I should do some introductions. Maile Spencer, this is Special Agent Michelle Hartzel of the FBI. Michelle, this is Maile Spencer, tour guide and registered nurse."

They shook hands. Doing her best not to stare, Maile tried seeing dark roots in Michelle's pale blond hair.

"Nice place," Michelle said.

"Thanks, but it's a dump. If you guys wait outside on the sidewalk for a few minutes, I can put on outdoor clothes."

Maile couldn't risk making them wait too long, if a meal was involved. The little bit of time she'd spent with David in the past had been pleasant, at the very least. He was single, handsome, kind, and well educated. A nephew to an ex-President, his pockets should be deep and lined with green. What wasn't to like? Face washed, hair brushed, and clothed in something colorful for the tour she needed to give later, she was downstairs before they had the chance to break into a sweat. When she got there, it was only the woman waiting for Maile.

"Where's David?"

"He had to go back to work. Where am I taking you?"

Maile stalled on the sidewalk. Without David, most of the fun of having breakfast was gone, and she was left with a woman that looked like she needed a vacation. "I thought this included him?"

"Mister Melendez has a very busy schedule, as do I, Miss Spencer. Let me assure you I'm quite harmless."

"It's Ms. Spencer, and as long as you have that pistol holstered to your body, you're not harmless. Not in my world."

"What world is that?"

"The world of an emergency room nurse."

"Are we eating breakfast or not?" the agent asked.

After loading into Hartzel's black four-wheel drive, Maile was careful to watch the direction they were headed, not to see where she was being taken for breakfast, but if it was to a federal office building in downtown Honolulu.

"This is all very mysterious," she said. "Why is a government agent taking a nobody like me to breakfast?"

"From what I've heard, you're anything but a nobody, Maile," Agent Hartzel said.

Honey of a Hurricane

She sat back, a little more relaxed after hearing her answer. At least she was being called Maile instead of Ms. Spencer.

They stopped at Willie's Waffle House in central Honolulu, in a part of town undiscovered by tourism. Buildings in the neighborhood were old, sidewalks were shaded by rickety awnings, and tree roots pushed up pavement. Old Japanese men crowded around tables in diners, each of them sipping from cups of coffee, 'talking story' about the good old days of Honolulu. Industrious young women ran small businesses, hoping to make ends meet while supporting extended families. The buses that served the area were used by kids going to and from school, old ladies on weekly shopping trips, and new immigrants learning their way around a tropical version of America. Other than the small house she grew up in, this was Maile's idea of home.

Willie's Waffles was an old family favorite. Maile's mother would take her and Kenny there on special occasions, usually birthdays or to celebrate a good report card. Sitting in a booth at the front window made it even more special for youngster Maile, because she would be seen having a meal in a restaurant. Just like the tattered awnings, broken sidewalks, and weather-stained walls in the neighborhood, Willie's had seen better days, but Maile was mostly blind to it.

Maile and the agent were shown to a booth in a back corner for privacy, something that seemed prearranged. Once they were seated, the waitress handed out menus and an insincere smile. After a quick look at the familiar menu, Maile ordered the largest platter of calories she could find, and even got a meal to go.

"You're eating breakfast again later, after this one?" Hartzel asked. "Where're you going to put it all?"

"I'll take it to my mother," Maile said. "What's all this about earning a little money on the side?"

Hartzel took over after their meals came. She ate quickly, making Maile wonder if all cops ate so fast.

"The federal government has an investigation going. Mister Melendez said you might be the perfect person to lend a hand with it."

"He knows me that well?"

"He seemed to," the agent said.

"Lend a hand? I know that means I'm already involved somehow."

"Miss Spencer, you know some of the primary players."

"Look, it's either Ms. Spencer or Maile, I don't care which. But I really don't like being called Miss Spencer."

"Okay, Maile. For several months, the FBI has been prepping an operation that the police would call a sting."

"You seriously want me to help federal agents with something? Because I've had enough trouble with…"

Hartzel put her hands up in surrender. "Does anybody in this town let anyone else do the talking?"

"Sorry."

"We have intelligence that there has been an abduction that involves someone you evidently know. That's why we're coming to you for help."

"Somebody's been kidnapped and you need a private citizen to help you get them back? Do I understand that correctly? I thought kidnappings were the business of the police?"

"Unless the victim is taken across state lines. We have solid intelligence that there are plans to take her to another state in the next two to three days. It might even involve the business of human trafficking."

"If you're talking about Prince Aziz and Mrs. Abrams, I have a guarantee from her that I am no longer involved in his case."

"I don't know who they are, but this has nothing to do with them."

Agent Hartzel paused long enough that Maile thought she had a chance to reply. "What's the word? You want me to infiltrate a gang of Vietnamese to get the inside scoop on their local operations? I came this close to dying at the hands of those guys a while back, a couple of times. No, thanks. My sense of civic duty ends when someone points a gun at me."

"There wouldn't be guns, and it isn't the Vietnamese we're worried about."

"Who is it, then?"

"I can't divulge that until I know you're signing on," Hartzel said.

Maile had a hard time swallowing what the agent was telling her. She put down her fork and took a slug of coffee to wash down her eggs. "I need to know who it is before I sign on."

"Maybe we can discuss the details a little more before you decide."

"I know a police detective who says the same thing about his investigations. The first couple of times I heard him say it, I was dumb enough to believe him. Honestly, I'd rather work with him than a federal agent. No offense meant."

"None taken. But a federal operation takes precedence over local law enforcement, Maile."

When Maile heard that, she knew Detective Ota, or someone with the local police department, had something to do with sending Hartzel to Maile for help. "So, use a federal agent to do your federal investigation."

"I'm getting the impression you're unwilling to be helpful to your nation," Hartzel said, pushing her half-eaten plate of food away.

Maile was finished with her meal and drank the last of her coffee. "Okay, seriously, you need to get to a point. What exactly would you expect from me?"

"You'd be at a home for a small, private party. The Bureau needs to know who shows up and interacts with others. You'd have to tread lightly, easing the group along in specific directions to…"

"I know. Social engineering. Special Agent, junior high school girls are experts at social engineering. By the age of fourteen, girls are able to pry anything out of anybody whenever we want. You just have to make it worth our while. Surely you remember how that worked?"

"I've heard you're handy at interrogation and counter-interrogation."

"You know, I really don't like that word. I'd rather think of it as getting some gossip, learning a few loosely held secrets."

"Whatever you want to call it, you're apparently the person we need. As you put it, you're able to pry information out of people without them realizing it, and you're familiar with the people involved. It would take me months to prep someone that well, and honestly, we don't have the time."

"You're forgetting two very important details. First, I'm not a trained agent. And second, I can't just knock on the front door and invite myself in."

"For the last time, you wouldn't need to be trained. I'd only want a few pictures, you know, selfies with other guests, and names to go with them. I'd handle the rest."

"The rest of what? It sounds like I'm the one doing all the heavy lifting, or at least taking most of the risks. Exactly what are you investigating?"

"We're not sure, but we think they have something to do with business dealings in California. That's why the Bureau is involved," Agent Hartzel said. "We just don't know what that business is, but there's a significant amount of money and a number of people involved. That's why this needs to be handled delicately."

"And instead of using an undercover cop, or whoever, you want me to do your dirty work and find out what that business is?"

"Right. Interested? Because I need a decision."

"Is there a hurry?" Maile asked.

"To an extent, yes. The longer we wait, the more changes and movement there is, and that only destabilizes the situation."

"How are you going to get me into the party without them being suspicious?" Maile asked. The investigation was intriguing, but she didn't like the idea of dealing with kidnappers. There were too many things that could go wrong with that.

"We know they've been having women come to the house…"

"Prostitutes?"

"They could possibly be that, yes. Each day, a new one comes by in the early afternoon. We'd intercept the one that has been summoned and have you take her place."

"You want me to…I'm supposed to…what's wrong with you?"

"Wait, let me explain."

"Yes, please do," Maile said blotting her lips now that her breakfast was done.

"We've talked to the others after they've left the house. They said the women that visit are there more as decoration, someone to talk to. Lounge lizards."

"They're there as entertainment? I see things going wrong with that."

"The sooner we can get you into that house, the more control we'll have over the situation."

When the waitress brought the bill and Maile's to-go meal wrapped in a bag, Maile gave the job some thought. "I get it. You already have an agent planted in the house, right?"

Hartzel seemed surprised. "What makes you think that?"

"If I were running an operation like yours, that's what I'd do. I'd plant someone in that spot, maybe not to interrogate someone, but just to keep an eye on things, and be an extra support person in case things went wrong."

Hartzel rubbed her forehead. "Never occurred to us. But as far as I know, there's no one there."

"So, you want me to go to party central, hangout for the day, sleep with whoever, get the dirt on sales of human beings, and not have anyone else around that might be on my team should trouble start?"

"Maybe a reward would be in order?" the agent offered.

"My body is not for sale, not to criminals, not to the federal government, not to anybody."

Chapter Three

There were two sites on the windward side of the island Maile was taking her tour to that day. Both had something to do with Hawaiian history and nature on the island, her favorite topics on tours. They rambled down a dirt road along one edge of the vast wetlands, bouncing through puddles and ruts.

"Our first stop is at the Kawai Nui Marsh, Hawaii's largest marshland. That simply means big swamp, which is what it is. We'll see many birds, both ones that live in the islands, along with migratory birds. Please stay out of the water, because many animals call that home. There are a couple of trails through the park, and we'll meet a lot of people out walking their dogs, going for jogs, or just out for fresh air. In the distance, you'll see the opposite side of the mountain range that you see from your hotels in Waikiki. They look entirely different on this side of the island."

"Greener on this side," someone said, once they were out of the van and on a walking tour. "And cloudier."

"This is the windward side of the island. They get twice as much rain on this side than in Honolulu."

"Which side do you like better, Maile?" one of the younger women asked.

"I grew up in Honolulu, so over there, I suppose. There are some important places near here that we'll see later that are near and dear to my heart, though."

They watched a young family fish in an open area of the marsh, and cheered on a little girl that hooked into a fish and reel it ashore. Nobody knew exactly what it was, but the father decided to keep it for dinner that evening.

"Many of these marshes were used by the Hawaiians for fishing and bird catching. They also built fishponds along the coastal areas. Each village had its own pond, and taro patches fed by streams coming down from the mountains. Between fish, birds, poi, pork, cane, and a few vegetables, they ate quite well."

"Do you eat poi?" someone asked.

"Maybe once a week or so. My mother buys it from a friend that sells it at a farmer's market. Otherwise, most supermarkets sell ready-made poi."

"Does it taste good?"

"It's an acquired taste. People who grow up with poi like it. Not many pick it up later on, though."

Discussing food was the perfect segway into their next stop.

"Our next stop is at the Ulupo Heiau. Does everybody know what a heiau is?" she asked as they rode along.

"Like a temple, right? Is that where they sacrificed virgins?"

"Well, they're temples, but let's not turn them into Hollywood movie sets. They're still considered sacred, and removal of any items, including rocks, is forbidden."

"But if nobody practices those old religions, why are they still considered sacred?" one of the men asked. He'd been asking the most questions, helping keep the discussion going at times.

"Think of it this way. In the Middle East and the Holy Lands, there are many churches and temples that haven't been used in hundreds of years, but those places are still considered sacred, right?"

"Yeah, but those are Christian places, or at least Jewish. The Hawaiians didn't practice a real religion, just that pagan stuff."

Lopaka and Maile shared a glance, Lopaka leaving her with a warning expression.

"Yes, well, let's treat the area with as much respect as we can, shall we?"

Maile took off her headset and tossed it on the dashboard, done with her lecture. She'd grown up going to a Christian church, with a small congregation attended mostly by Hawaiians. But she also felt strongly about the religion of her heritage. She was equally comfortable offering prayers at a heiau as she was in a church.

After asking her group to wait at the first set of signs while they exited the bus, she looked at Lopaka. "If just one of them swipes a stone off that heiau, I'll…"

"You'll take it back and replace it where it belongs, and that'll be the end of it, Mai."

"We'll see. There might be a silent prayer for a curse or two."

Maile caught up with her group of a dozen, the largest size she could take on tours because of seating in the van. Most were busy snapping pictures of the heiau and surrounding area with phones, while the oldest in the group was setting up his tripod and impressive camera with a long lens. The others were already reading the interpretive signs, which was cheating in Maile's view.

A couple of ditches flowed through the area, feeding small, swampy taro patches. Other plots were growing leafy vegetables or cane. Simple display huts had been built from poles, with woven mats as walls and thatched roofs. A man was sitting in the shade of one weaving a hat from long, slender hala leaves. All of it sat at the base of a massive stone mound.

"This is one of the inland villages. It was considered inland, even though it's only a short walk to the beach. They didn't use canoes to fish, but traded kalo with coastal villages for ocean fish."

"What's kalo?"

"The real word for taro. If you walk this way, and stay on the walking paths, you'll find taro patches. All of these tiny ponds were fed by streams. Pigs and dogs would live in the villages, never roaming far. When one village had an excess of something, they would take it to another village, hoping to make a trade for what they needed. Villages became well-known for having cottage industries, such as sea salt production, or raising certain kinds of fish in their ponds."

A few raindrops hit. Maile considered putting up her umbrella, but figured no one else had them.

"Wow, I bet the weather really played a big part in how they lived back then," someone said.

"They were very tuned into the weather, able to forecast quite accurately what kind of weather they were going to have, often days in advance. It was a very outdoor lifestyle."

She let the group divide up how they wanted and wander the area. Once she was alone at the heiau, Lopaka brought a bag to her.

"Keep an eye on them for me, brah." She opened the bag and took out a simple lei. "Don't let them wander too far off."

"How long do you need?" he asked.

"Ten minutes should be okay. I'll be on the other side of the heiau, so they won't see me."

With the maile vine lei in one hand, and a plastic shopping bag in the other, she took off at a run around one side of the massive stone temple. It was mostly a giant platform of stacked lava stones with a flat top, fairly simple. But Maile was one of the few people who was allowed to climb to the low elevation at the top. The only things up there were an upright stone altar, and a small hut made from tree branches with palm fronds as a roof. After she made the quick scramble to the top, she went to the hut first.

"Brother Kakuhihewa, are you there?" she said in Hawaiian.

"Who's that come here?" someone mumbled back.

"It's Hokuhoku'ikalani."

The hanging mat that served as the door was folded aside. A heavy man with white chest hair and a thick white batch of hair on his head, a red and brown kapa sarong wrapped around his hips looked out from the shade of the hut. "Kamali'i-wahine Hokuhoku'ikalani?"

She took him the bag of groceries. "Store bought. I hope you don't mind?"

The old man's face brightened when he looked inside the bag. "You always get it right."

"Something special for you in there. Better wait for nighttime to drink it."

"What brings our favorite princess to Ulupo?"

Maile smiled and nearly blushed. "I don't know about her, but I'm here to leave something for our ancestors." She held up the lei. "Is it okay?"

"Of course! They will be glad to know you came for a visit."

She took the vine lei to the stone alter and hung it from the top. Raising her hands toward the sky, she said a quick prayer, before going back to the old man in his hut.

"Brother, do you need anything the next time I visit?"

"Only a visit from my favorite princess. When will you sit down with me to share poi and fish?"

"I hope next time, Brother. But I have haoles waiting for me."

"Go, treat them well," he said. He seemed to give something great consideration. "Except one will break the kapu of the heiau."

"I'll be careful with them," she said, before hurrying off. On her way back, she wondered what kapu, or forbidden act, she should watch for. It could be as simple as accidently trespassing, or egregious as stealing a sacred object. Once she was back to the meeting place, Lopaka was taking pictures of the group with several cameras.

"What are all these plants with the long leaves?" the man full of curiosity asked. He was examining one of the plants. "Some are red and others are green. They go all the way around the pile of rocks."

"Those are ti plants. They circle the temple because they're one of the sacred plants of Hawaii and Polynesia. Many people have them in their landscaping, thinking of them as protective of the home and family."

The man pulled out a pocketknife and before she could stop him, cut a leaf off a tall stem.

"Ah!" Maile yelled. She took the leaf from him. "Please don't do that. These plants, this whole area is very important to the local people."

"Just a park with a big pile of rocks," the man said, walking away.

Not caring if anyone was watching, Maile went to the closest side of the heiau, found an appropriate rock, wrapped the ti leaf around it, and set the rock back with all the others.

"What kapu comes next?" she muttered, as she went past Lopaka to catch up with her group.

"They need a lot of supervision," he whispered back.

"One of them needs to go back to his hotel before he finds trouble."

When she caught up with them, a discussion about how the temple was built and where the rocks came from was being argued.

"That's a fun question to answer. Maybe you've heard of the menehune?" Maile asked.

"Those little guys that hide in the forest?"

"There's more to their legend than that. Supposedly the menehune were very powerful, and could lift many times their own weight. They were talented builders of temples, fishponds, and canals, often completing an entire project in only one go. They worked only at night, when humans weren't around. But if they thought they were being watched, they'd quit working and leave, never to return to the project."

"I think the place was built by a crew with bulldozers and cranes."

Honey of a Hurricane

Maile ignored the man. "All of these rocks came from several miles away, and had to be carried here one at a time. Five hundred years ago…" She made the point of saying that. "…when this temple was built, they had no carts or the wheel, or animals strong enough to carry these stones."

"And trucks," the man said.

"I'm utterly amazed whenever I visit a heiau," Maile said, finishing the talk.

"Yeah, amazing pile of rocks."

"Sir…" Maile started.

"Mai, time to go," Lopaka said, hurriedly.

A gentle rain was beginning to fall, the kind that Maile would expect on that side of the island. Normally those little squalls were calming to her, but not that day. Clamping her molars together, she turned the group back in the direction of the van. She got to the door before they could, and positioned so they couldn't enter without passing her.

"Okay, ladies and gentlemen. Before heading home, I just need to take a quick look in your bags to make sure something from the heiau or park didn't accidentally fall in."

One by one, each was inspected before boarding the van. The man that had been giving Maile and Lopaka such a hard time all day was the last to enter.

"I don't have a bag," he said, trying to get past her. He was the one she was most worried about.

"What's that in your pocket?"

He reached in for a weather-beaten lava stone. "Nothing. Just a rock."

"It's from the heiau, isn't it?"

"I found it on the ground."

"It's too clean to have been on the ground." She took it from his hand. "Where are you from?"

"Pennsylvania."

"Isn't that where Gettysburg Battlefield is?" she asked.

"Yeah, so?"

"What if someone stole something from there? Would you be upset?"

"To say the least!"

"Why?' she asked.

"Because Gettysburg is hallowed ground!"

"Exactly. So is the heiau. Get on the bus."

Maile took the stone back to the heiau. Knowing she was being watched, she replaced the rock while whispering a simple prayer asking for forgiveness. By the time she got back to the van, more trouble had started with the man.

"I lost my wallet!" he was saying over and over.

"When was the last time you had it?" one of the women on the tour asked.

"I had it when we got here. Someone picked my pocket!"

Maile had Lopaka open the door again. "I'll give you five minutes to go look for it. Just be sure to look for the wallet and not another rock."

Most of the guests looked at each other's pictures on phones, while Maile watched the man to make sure he didn't swipe another stone. When he boarded again griping about pickpockets and the tourism industry in general but without his wallet, Maile had a pretty good idea of what happened.

"You know where his wallet is?" she asked Lopaka as he got the van started.

"No idea."

"Either do I." She put on her headset and turned the sound system on. "And that's why we don't mess with sacred places. Please take your seats and enjoy the ride back to sunny Waikiki."

Chapter Four

Maile had only the one tour of windward sites to give that afternoon and couldn't get home fast enough. As soon as she was, she changed into jogging clothes and went for a long run. At just over an hour of pressing her pace as much as she physically could, it was her longest run in years. But when she trotted down her block, she didn't like what she saw in front of her building.

Maile felt like she was being watched as she slowed to a walk. A dark blue sedan was parked in front of her building. One person was inside, at the steering wheel. It wasn't Detective Ota, but it reeked of being some sort of cop.

Tapping a finger on her sports watch, she checked her time and heart rate. For all intents and purposes, her workout had been a success. Except for whoever it was that was watching her from the car.

Instead of going into her apartment building, Maile went to the car's passenger window, keeping a couple of steps back. The windows were up, and being tinted, she couldn't see much of the driver. Still, the woman looked familiar. When the window went down, she got a better look. After a moment, she realized who it was.

"You're Maile Spencer, right?" the blonde asked.

"That's right. You're that agent that watches over Mayor Kato over on Maui. I'm sorry, but I don't remember your name."

"Agent Cassandra Smith. Do you have a few minutes to talk?"

Maile used the front of her T-shirt to wipe sweat from her face. "Just getting in from a long run. Maybe another time."

"This is important."

"Why? Is Thérèse okay? Did something happen to her?"

Cassandra smiled slightly. "She's fine. She keeps talking about how she wants to come back to Honolulu to see her hanai sister, Maile. But that's not what I need to talk to you about."

"What, then?"

"I need your help with something."

Maile took a step toward the car. "With?"

"It's something that needs to be discussed in private."

"Oh, yes. You're from the Secret Service. What do you guys want with me? You don't think I'm a threat to Doctor Kato, do you?"

"No, nothing to do with her. Can you give me a few minutes?" Cassandra asked. She had been on Melanie Kato's personal protection detail for years, because as daughter of an ex-President, Melanie got Secret Service protection as a young woman. Periodically, that protection was renewed. Most of the time it wasn't necessary, but there had been times in the last few years that Cassandra's protection had come in handy.

Maile pointed down the street. "There's a teriyaki place around the corner. I'll meet you there."

"I can give you a ride."

"Thanks, I'd rather walk."

Maile got to the homey little diner before Cassandra could drive there and park. When they went inside, the agent looked at the menu.

"I'm not planning to eat. Just something cold to drink," Maile said.

"Already eaten dinner?"

Maile leaned close to whisper. "No. It's just a little risky to eat the food they serve here, but the fountain drinks are okay."

She paid the proprietor for two sodas and went to a table near the door.

"Might be better if we sat in the corner," Cassandra said.

"Right here is fine. What did you want to talk with me about?"

Cassandra sat stiffly. "As you know, I work for the Secret Service. One of the roles of our agency is to assist in the investigation of the production and use of counterfeit US currency. In the past, it was a much bigger role for us. Now the Treasury Department is responsible for counterfeiting."

"Why are you telling me this?"

"Here in Hawaii, federal agencies are stretched thin, and we need to rely on each other for help from time to time. Because of that, we still lend a hand to Treasury agents whenever we can."

"Okay, I'm not a threat to Melanie Kato, I pay my fair share of taxes, and I'm not making funny money on a printing press in my bathroom. I don't know why the federal government is interested in me."

"There's a joint investigation between the Service and the Treasury Department into what you call funny money."

"You think I'm passing fake twenties? Because the cash I get paid at the tour agency comes from Thomas, the owner of the place. You need to talk to him about where it comes from."

Cassandra shook her head. "Not about you passing twenties, although a part of the problem is with larger bills, usually fifties and hundreds. Our concern is where they're coming from, and who is moving them."

"And I'm supposed to know?" Maile asked.

"No. We have a pretty good idea of who might be moving some in the next few days, or at least where. We just need help in identifying that person, and witnessing the exchange of goods for money."

"You have pictures for me to look at of known counterfeiters? I don't know anybody like that."

"Not pictures. We'd need you to be present when the money is passed from one hand to the other."

"Why me? I don't know anything about fake money," Maile said.

"You don't need to. The investigating team only needs you to see the exchange. If you happened to get a bill as an example, that would be great."

"It sounds like an undercover operation. What do you want me to do that can't be done by an agent?"

"We're concerned that all the agents in Hawaii could be recognized, and we can't get an agent here from the mainland and prepped in time."

"In time for what?"

"The exchange is supposed to take place in the next couple of nights, most likely tomorrow night."

"It's only a five hour flight from the west coast to here. It would take longer than that to prep me. Why not use a professional?"

"We need you," the agent said.

Maile took her cup to the soda fountain for a refill. While she was there, she wasted time by drying the sweat from the outside of the cup. Getting a fresh napkin, she wrapped the large cup with that. The whole time, she wondered why the Secret Service wanted her to help with an investigation that involved counterfeit money. Even more, she wondered who put them onto her trail. It couldn't have been Detective Ota, because he wasn't any fonder of federal agents than Maile was, nor did he have much to do with counterfeiters.

"Mrs. Abrams put you up to this, didn't she?" Maile asked, sitting down again.

"Mrs. Abrams?"

"She's the federal prosecutor in Honolulu, US District Attorney, whatever the right word is. Does Prince Aziz have something to do with the counterfeit money?"

"I have no idea who Prince Aziz is, or Mrs. Abrams. I'm not here about them," Cassandra said.

"Who put you up to this? Who sent you to me?"

"Thérèse, actually. Maybe not directly, but it was how you managed the situation at Diamond Head a while back, the discretion you used that time. I also knew that Detective Ota and you cross paths occasionally. So, I went to him and asked about you possibly helping us. There are a few other factors about this investigation, but that's the brunt of it."

"Detective Ota sent you to me?" Maile asked, surprised.

"Maybe it wasn't exactly sent. He said you might be interested in helping."

"I'll have to talk to him about that."

"We're willing to pay you. It would be reward money, completely legitimate."

"I'm supposed to pretend to be some junior agent and spy on a counterfeiting operation, without any training? How much are you willing to pay for my amateur services?"

The agent had a business card already to go with a number on the back. She pushed it across the table to Maile.

It took only a glance to know it wasn't enough. As much as she needed money, there could never be enough to do dirty work for federal agents. Maile pushed it back. She stood from their small table and pushed her chair in. "I hope you catch your counterfeiter."

Chapter Five

The next morning, Maile called Detective Ota to find out why he sent the Secret Service agent to her.

"I didn't send her to you, Maile. I got a call from her the other day to see if I had someone that could lend a hand with an undercover job."

"How did my name get mixed up in it?" she asked.

"I gave her a couple of names, not yours. Then she chatted me up about life and times in Honolulu, and that eventually turned into you taking the Kato kid on that tour a while back. By the time I figured out she was working me into a corner, I'd let on too much. Sorry."

Maile couldn't hide her sigh. "Don't worry about it. She was working on me pretty hard, waving money in my face."

"How much?" he asked.

"Not nearly enough."

"Since I have you on the phone, I do have something to talk to you about."

"About that guest who lost his wallet yesterday?"

"Who's that?" he asked.

"Some guy was disrespecting the heiau over in Kailua yesterday and lost his wallet."

"Did you help him look for it?" Ota asked.

"We gave him a chance to find it. When he didn't, I chalked it up to cosmic payback. What do you want to talk to me about?"

"Are you busy this weekend?"

"Still not interested in dating. Not you, not Turner, not anyone until my divorce papers finally come through."

"I thought they had a while back?" Ota asked.

"That idiot husband of mine decided to contest one or two little things. I thought you put Robbie in a jail cell?"

"Another detective is working his case. From what I've heard, he's low priority right now."

"I'd like to high priority my foot in his…"

"You're really hung up on not dating until the papers are signed, aren't you?"

"Getting to the point, Detective, yes, even if I am lonely and not busy this weekend."

"Care to help me out with something and make a few bucks in the process?"

"Pretend to be a hooker in Chinatown to catch my friend Suzie Face Slap in the act?"

Ota laughed. "No. She's easy enough to find. But it would involve a few hours of dressing well and possibly being flirtatious."

"Listen carefully," she hissed. "I'm not dating."

"Not a date, and perfectly legit. Mostly. Can you listen with a mind open to helping out the police department? It involves you, in a round-about way."

"This is about the Swenbergs, isn't it?" she asked.

"Very intuitive. I'm still trying to solve that murder case. Two murder cases, in fact."

"I don't know any more than what I told you and the other investigating officers about either Frank or Carl's murder. I don't see how I can be helpful at all."

"I'm not going to beat around the bush with this. You're too smart for that. Maile, what I need is someone to go to Oscar Swenberg's house, similar to an undercover operation. If you agreed, I'd want you to talk with both Oscar and Honey, to find out what they know about the murders, if anything."

"I thought you already had him in jail?" she asked.

"I had to kick him loose a while back. The DA felt like we didn't have enough evidence to bring charges. That's what I need from you, to see if there could be more evidence linking him to the murders, or no evidence which would clear him."

"I'm not a skilled investigator, Detective. I'm not even a snitch, or whatever you call Lenny."

"I haven't seen Lenny around for a while, and he wouldn't be useful for this operation anyway. But in many ways, you are skilled. You know how to pry information out of people without them suspecting anything."

"I can get gossip, not evidence."

"That's all I need, gossip. One of our usual tactics is to get one person to gossip about another, to the point of divulging something useful. If you can then turn it around and verify that with the other, that's even better. That's when you take a hike and clear out. Interested?"

Maile wanted the Swenberg investigation behind her as much as Ota wanted it solved. Maybe it was time to get a little more involved? Investing a few hours on a day off to wipe that slate clean might be worth it. "You said something about money?"

"The police department is not wealthy, Maile."

"Either am I. If you want my help, come up with a decent number to make it worth my time and risk."

"How much is your rent?"

"A little personal, isn't it?"

"Just appease me," he said.

She told him. "Even a dump like this place is expensive in Honolulu."

"I can cover next month's rent."

To Maile, that was a lot, more than what she earned as a tour guide most weeks. "I want an expense account to buy an outfit I can wear to a place in Hawaii Kai."

"Forget it. Money for rent. That's it."

"Okay, how about this. I want a get out of jail free card for anything and everything related to the Swenberg case, now and forever more."

"That's asking a lot. I can't do that as a cop. The DA is the one who makes deals like that."

"Okay, find Lenny the snitch and have him wear a dress to the Swenberg's house."

There was a pause, until, "Okay, you have your hall pass. With the Swenberg case only."

"When am I supposed to go there?"

"Today."

"Today? Believe it or not, I have a life, Detective Ota."

"You have a tour to give this afternoon?"

"No, but…"

"A date?"

"I'm not at your beck and call, that I can just drop whatever I'm doing to do whatever you want me to do," Maile said. "That's what those girls are for that hang around Chinatown street corners."

"I know that's short notice, but there's a bit of a rush on this deal. Something's up with Honey, we're not sure of what. She might be taking a flyer soon, and we need you to talk to her before she does."

"And now those fake passports for them that I found hidden in the yacht a while back are causing you some concern?" she asked.

"Causing a lot of concern for a lot of people."

"How do you know she might be taking off?" Maile asked.

"We've heard she has a bag packed, a large suitcase as if she's not planning on coming back."

"A full suitcase means a long trip, not just to another island. Where exactly is she going?"

"Probably back to LA."

"That's right. I forgot she spent a few years there before coming back to Honolulu. Is Oscar going with her?"

"Oscar had an accident a while back, not long after we cut him loose. I doubt he's going anywhere for a while."

"Two brothers murdered, the third in bad shape. Some pretty bad juju going around in that family. What happened to him?"

"We're not sure what happened, but we've had the house staked out off and on for a while. We did see him get brought home from the hospital with both legs in casts and his arm in some fancy sling. Ever since then, a woman has been staying there with them, we think a private duty nurse. Anyway, our primary focus is on Honey for now."

"How do you expect to get me into his house?" she asked. "I can't just walk up to his front door and ask to be let in."

"That's where you might need to put on a little show, basically the same as you did a while back at his party."

"He's holding a party, even when he's in a wheelchair?"

"No. Maybe there's some pre-marital discord between Oscar and Honey, but each afternoon for the last few days, a young lady of questionable charms...that's how you put it, right?...has been going to the Swenberg house for a few hours. What we want to do is intercept her, and replace her with you for one day."

"That's exactly what your friend the fed said to me at breakfast the other day. She wanted me to trade places with a hooker and spend the afternoon entertaining at the Swenberg house."

"Agent Hartzel?" he asked. "She got that far with you, to explain what we want?"

"Oh, so you're working together?"

"Minimally. She gave me a call and asked me to talk with you about it again."

"I told her I'd think about it."

"Did you? She said she never heard back from you?" Ota asked.

"I thought about it for five whole minutes, before deciding I still didn't like federal agents very much. I guess I'm not as red, white, and true blue as you think I am." Maile knew that was an excuse. She felt as patriotic as anyone, despite what the US government had done to her ancestors a century before. She was more concerned with being able to function at the level of deceitful sophistication that they wanted. It was one thing to pry gossip out of doctors and nurses; dealing with the criminal element was something else. "Okay, so this is weird. Oscar is in a wheelchair. He has Honey, his main squeeze and primary bimbo, but he needs to bring in outside help for…whatever?"

"He also has that nurse there."

Maile's hackles were up. "Contrary to what they put in movies, nurses don't do that sort of thing with patients, Detective."

"Just relax. That's not how I meant it. What I meant was that being in a wheelchair with his legs in casts and a nurse tending to his care means he's not getting services provided to him. The women are going there for some other reason."

"Maybe someone else is there?" she asked.

"Could be. They have their groceries delivered, and the amount looks about right for feeding three people, maybe one or two more. Our stakeout team hasn't seen anyone go in or out of the house except for the women each afternoon."

"Doesn't Honey go out?"

"Not that we've seen, not since she brought Oscar home from the hospital. She's either been playing the role of dutiful wife and staying by his side, or left when we weren't looking. If that's the case, you could focus on Oscar."

"I'd rather not see her anyway."

"So, you'll do it? You'll help me out?" Ota asked.

"Look pal, if you burn me on this deal, I'll make you regret it. And you better believe I can figure out a way of doing that."

Ota laughed. "I know you can, too!"

Honey of a Hurricane

***

Maile went to the police station early the next morning as Ota had requested. He wanted to do some prep work with her, and had promised it would be fun. He also promised that he was running the operation, and not Agent Hartzel. Once she was seated at his desk, he excused himself to get coffee for her. Once she was sipping, he left her again, coming back a few minutes later, bringing someone with him. It was a young Asian woman with jet-black glossy hair, too much makeup, and an outfit that revealed more body jewelry than it hid. Maile had met her a few times before.

"Schoolteacher," the girl said to Maile as a greeting.

"Why is she here?" Maile asked Ota.

"Suzie's going to help you prep."

"Prep how? Teach me the latest moves in bed? Because I'd rather figure them out on my own."

"Hey!" Suzie glared at Ota. "Nobody said I was gonna be picked on!"

"You're not being picked on," he said.

"Actually, I was just getting started with picking on her," Maile said.

"Can the two of you bury the hatchet for a few minutes while we figure this thing out?"

Maile and Suzie did the exact same thing in folding their arms over their chests and bounce a foot impatiently.

"Maile, Suzie has been one of the girls I told you about that's been to the Swenberg house."

"You expect me to transform into that?" Maile said, nodding her head in Suzie's direction.

"Hey!"

"I don't expect you to transform into anything. I do need you to wear a different outfit, but not yet. I want her to tell you about what's going on there."

"I think I can figure that out on my own."

"Watch it, Schoolteacher. I don't need to be here today."

"No, you need to be in a clinic somewhere getting a penicillin shot."

With that, Suzie sprang from her seat and tackled Maile to the floor. Along with a couple other cops that had been passing by, Ota was on top of both of them, pulling them apart. It hadn't been much of a battle, but Maile came away with a black wig in her hand.

"Gimme that!" Suzie shouted.

"Quiet down or you're going back in the cage," Ota told her.

After looking at the wig, Maile looked at Suzie back in her chair. "What happened to you?"

"I shaved my head, okay? I had to, after you started pulling it out a while back. Gimme my wig!"

"Wasn't my fault it was falling out on its own."

"Gimme my wig!"

"Not till you promise to be nice."

"Yeah, whatever."

"And stop calling me schoolteacher."

"You never told me your name," Suzie said.

"Never had the chance! You were always picking a fight with me."

Ota had been watching the verbal tennis match. "Suzie, remember the deal we made. Maile, give back Suzie's hair."

Maile handed over the wig, which Suzie combed with her fingers.

"Your head looks good like that," Maile said.

"What's that supposed to mean?"

"It just does, okay? It's not all lumpy."

"Thanks. I guess."

"Okay, great. Now that we're all friends again, can we talk about Swenberg?" Ota asked.

"With you?" Suzie said with a sneer.

"Why not with me? This is my operation," he said.

"We don't need a referee," Maile said.

"The two of you need a warden." Ota took out his wallet and gave Maile a twenty. "There's a fast food place across the street where you can talk."

"Where's mine?" Suzie said, with her hand out.

"Maile's buying."

"I need my stuff," Suzie griped.

"You'll get it when you come back to the station. Consider yourself still in jail."

When Maile bolted for the door, Suzie chased after. "Hey! Half of that is mine!"

Maile did her best to leave Suzie behind, even jaywalking across the busy boulevard that fronted the police station. Suzie kept up, though, in her giant wedge clogs, carrying her wig in one hand. After getting sodas, they sat at a table in a corner.

"What goes on at Swenberg's house if it's not what I think it is?" Maile asked once their détente was hammered out and Suzie had her wig on again.

"Nothing. There's this girl there…"

"Honey?"

"Right. She spends most of her time drinking. Then there's a nurse that takes care of the guy."

"What does she do for him?"

"I don't know. Helps him with stuff, pushes him around in his chair. I don't know what goes on when I'm not there."

Maile wasn't sure why, but she got the feeling that Suzie was withholding something. "Why does Swenberg want you there, if it isn't for favors?"

"It's like, I dunno, he just wants someone different to talk to. Honey's blasted most of the time and the nurse never talks at all. She's always hanging around listening, but never says much."

"What's Swenberg talk about?" Maile asked.

"Not much. His boat, mostly. Money a couple of times."

"What about money?" Maile asked.

"Like he needs it. For a rich guy with a fancy house and a boat, he sure needs more money."

To Maile, it sounded pretty boring, just another day cooped up in the house doing nothing. No small wonder they were getting girls to come in each day. Swenberg needed fresh ears to talk to. "What else goes on in the house?"

"Not much. Yesterday, his nurse gave him a pill and he fell asleep. Pain pill, I guess. Got him snockered, anyway. Not long after that, Honey…" Suzie stopped and looked up at Maile.

"Honey what?"

"Nothing."

"I don't understand why they have someone like you go to the house, just to sit and talk, or to watch him sleep."

"Either do I, okay?" Suzie said. "Easy money, so I don't complain."

"That's it, then? You didn't have to perform?"

"Kept all my clothes on. Why're you doing this for the cops? What does Ota have on you that he's making you do this for him?"

"He doesn't have anything on me. He just needs a favor to help solve a crime."

"What did Swenberg do? Kill someone?"

"Maybe," Maile said.

"Who?"

"His brothers."

Suzie sat back in her chair. "Dang, that's a tough family."

"Do you know what kind of accident he was in?"

Suzie nodded. "It weren't no accident."

Maile looked around the fast food place. "What happened to him?"

"The nurse said someone got rough with him."

"Was it something to do with Ota's investigation?"

The girl shrugged. "She didn't say anything about who or why, but there's someone out there that really don't like that Swenberg guy."

"Anything else you can tell me about what's going on between Oscar and Honey?"

Another shrug. "She sits at the bar stoned on booze, and he sits in his wheelchair stoned on pain pills. The nurse hung around looking officious while I just sat there talking about whatever nonsense I thought of to Swenberg. Otherwise…never mind."

"And you got paid?" Maile asked.

"Two hundred, cash, fifties, new bills."

"Is that why you're in jail today?"

"Look, I work hard, you know? I have to hustle if I want to keep up my rep on the streets. If I did just one job a day, I wouldn't have a bank account."

"You have money in the bank?"

"Sure. Why wouldn't I?"

"I don't know much about what you…about your line of work," Maile muttered.

"Look, Schoolteacher. With your face and body, you could do good. Get a new hairstyle and some new clothes, you could work downtown bars pulling in five hundred, maybe even eight hundred a day."

"What's wrong with my clothes?"

"Nothing, if you like looking like a school teacher."

***

While they talked in the fast food diner, rain started and the usual trades were picking up a notch into steady wind. When they got back to Ota's desk at the police station, Suzie's personal belongings were waiting for her. She didn't even slow down when grabbing them and heading for the exit. "See you later, Schoolteacher. Have fun this afternoon."

"The two of you bond?" Ota asked, chuckling.

"No fistfights, anyway. Now what happens?"

He got a shopping bag of clothes for her. "Put these on. It's almost time to go."

Maile looked at the halter-top blouse. It was her size but not her style. "Whose is this?"

"It's used by female officers during stings. It's been laundered."

She gave it a sniff. "I have to look the part?"

"Right. The ladies room is through that door and down the hall. There's some makeup in there and hair spray to use. If you need help, I'll find an officer for you."

"I can dress myself. But when I went there for that party a while back, I was dressed well. Do you expect them to not recognize me dressed in this stuff?"

"I'm hoping they do. Creating a little bit of confusion will put them off. It'll be a good ice breaker, something to talk about."

Maile looked at the tiny skirt she was expected to wear. "More of a belt than a skirt."

"Will it fit?" he asked.

"I'm worried about the buttons and a wardrobe malfunction."

"You know what to look like?" he asked.

"I'll channel my inner Suzie."

After closing herself into the bathroom stall, Maile put on the denim miniskirt and the form-fitting canary yellow halter-top. It wasn't much more than running clothes, but somehow made her feel cheap. One thing she often wore was a simple, sheer silk scarf that she tied around her neck, serving as nothing more than a decorative accessory. Using a comb to rat some of her hair, she sprayed that into position before working on makeup. When she had four times as much on as she would wear for a hot date, she figured she was done and returned to Detective Ota.

"How do I look?"

"Cheap."

Maile looked down at her body trapped inside the outfit. "Really?"

"Don't worry. You're supposed to."

"Okay, who's taking me to Hawaii Kai?"

"Nobody. You'll need to drive yourself."

"My car's been on the blink for a couple of weeks. I seriously doubt a hooker would show up at a luxury place in an old bucket of bolts anyway."

"Can't risk someone seeing you leave the station with me," Ota said.

"Then how am I supposed to get there?"

"Take the bus to the transit center. I'll pick you up in an unmarked sedan and take you the rest of the way."

"I'm supposed to ride the bus looking like this? What if someone I know sees me?"

Ota left her alone for a moment to talk with a female officer. She left, and a moment later returned with a large hat with a floppy brim and large, round sunglasses.

"Wear this," he said, giving Maile the hat and glasses.

"It's too cloudy for sunglasses." Once again, Maile smelled the inside of the hat.

"Wear them anyway. She doesn't have fleas, if that's what you're worried about." He opened a drawer for something. "Put on some of this."

Maile gave the small bottle a sniff. "You keep Tabu perfume in your desk?"

"You know what Tabu smells like?"

"Every woman does. Story is that it was made for ladies practicing suspicious professions. I'm supposed to wear this?"

"You're playing a part, remember?"

"Tabu is what Suzie wears to hide…whatever."

"I know what Suzie smells like. Just put some on."

Maile rubbed a little on her wrists and gave back the bottle. "Maybe I should roll around in a dirty bed like Suzie does all day."

"You really don't like each other, do you?" he asked.

"Let's see. She's given me a bloody nose, and I've pulled out some of her hair. We don't like each other's career choices, how the other dresses, hairstyles, taste in men, or lifestyles. I'm pretty sure she needs a shot of penicillin in the rear end, and I'd like to give it to her. Not much common ground."

Ota laughed. "Did you bring anything that can be identified as belonging to Maile Spencer?"

"Just my phone."

"You'll need that to call me to come pick you up."

"Where're you going to be if there's trouble?"

"Not far away. Patrol also knows there's an undercover operation in Hawaii Kai this afternoon. Remember, you're Mary Spellman again, not Maile Spencer. Whatever you do, don't react to the wrong name."

"Something's going wrong, I know it," Maile said, headed for the exit.

"Maile?"

"Yes?"

"You don't have to do this thing. Are you sure you want to?"

"Not completely, no."

***

The hour-long city bus ride to Hawaii Kai was the first she'd been on since being in an accident on the same route a few weeks before. She was healed up and mostly over it, except cringing internally whenever the bus driver needed to make a hard stop. The group in the back of the bus looked a little too rough for her tastes, especially for the way she was dressed that day. Keeping the exit door in view, Maile decided to sit near the front.

The usual assortment of riders got on, an old Chinese lady with too many grocery bags that made herself at home in the handicap seats, a pair of teenaged boys that made wisecracks about Maile as they went by, and a tourist couple. The husband was pulled down the aisle toward the back by his wife when he tried sitting behind Maile. When a young mother got on with her little girl, the girl hopped into a seat directly across from Maile. But when the mother spotted Maile in her get-up, she took the girl to another seat.

Maile felt like a sociologic research subject on the bus ride, with the way people looked at and treated her. By the end of the ride, she had a whole new perspective of how Suzie must be treated wherever she went.

As the bus pulled into the transit center, Maile saw Ota parked in a dark sedan that looked freshly washed and polished. She also saw something she didn't like one bit: two police cars that were waiting there.

The two cops blocked the path of the bus. One went to the driver's window while the other climbed aboard, not allowing anyone to exit. Maile was in one of the first seats back from the door and got a hard look from the officer before he moved on down the aisle.

"Is there a problem, officer?" the driver asked.

"Looking for a couple of Filipino brothers named Bautista. Allegedly robbed a bank downtown a couple hours ago and they were last seen taking a bus in this direction. We're checking all the buses." The officer showed the driver a picture. "Look familiar?"

"Look like twins."

"Yeah, but do they look familiar? Have they been on your route?"

"Not that I noticed. I don't look at the riders, only at their bus passes."

Maile watched as the other cop on the bus came back to the front. He shook his head at his partner before getting off.

"Yeah, if you see them, don't say anything to them. Don't be a hero. Just give us a call at 9-1-1 after you drop them off so we know where they are."

Maile was the first off the bus and made a beeline to the restrooms, where she checked her makeup. Pulling off her hat, she ratted her hair a little more. With any luck, Honey or Oscar might not even recognize her from the party she'd attended at their place a few weeks before. When she came out, the bus was gone, as were most of the passengers that she'd ridden with. Ota was still there, waiting with the engine running and the A/C turned on.

"What did those two want?" Ota asked, once Maile was in the car.

"Something about a bank robbery downtown and they used a bus as a getaway car. You guys still call it a getaway car? Or is that just in the movies?"

He delayed in leaving the parking lot. "You watch too many movies."

"We don't seem to be going anywhere."

"We need to talk."

"About?" she asked. Maile knew enough about Detective Ota that when he said they needed to talk, it was unavoidable.

"There's something about this setup, this operation, that isn't quite right."

"Oh, there's definitely something fishy about it."

"What's bothering you about it?" he asked.

"First, what's the deal with Oscar getting beat up to the point of needing casts?"

"Where'd you hear that?" Ota asked.

"Suzie. She also said Honey was depressed and spending most of her time cuddling a bottle, rather than Oscar. That's entirely different from when I met them a while back."

"That's been bothering me also. Anything else?"

"Yeah, a lot. Swenberg has a private duty nurse that doesn't seem to accomplish anything, other than being a companion to him. What's up with that?"

"I hear you," he said.

"And just exactly why isn't he in a hospital bed if he's in such bad shape? That doesn't make sense at all."

"That's what I've been thinking."

"So, I'm not nuts for thinking all those things? That there's a lot more to this little afternoon affair than meets my eye?"

"Not nuts at all. I do think it's a little nutty that you agreed to help so readily."

"Maybe. But I need the money. I also want to dig into Swenberg's life. I still think he had something to do with his brothers' deaths. Maybe spending the day at his house I can find the knife that was used to kill his brother. Or maybe just get some sort of confession out of him after he's had a pain pill for his broken legs, washed down by his afternoon cocktail."

"Today is more about the Swenberg murders for you than it is about earning some money?"

"Ninety percent about the murders. The money is icing on the cake."

"What about Brock Turner?"

"What about him? He's not a part of this stupid job…stakeout, whatever."

"I was wondering more about your interest level in him," Ota said.

Maile gave the man, and their three almost dates, some thought. "I haven't seen him around lately. Maybe that ship has passed."

"If you're interested in sailing that ship, you might want to get your own boat in the water, if you know what I mean." With a lurch, Detective Ota started on the last leg of her journey to the Swenberg house.

"Why? Do you know something I don't?"

"There might be other boats in his harbor these days. Or maybe I'm a hopeless romantic. But for the next few hours, keep your head screwed on tight, Maile. If you need to get out early because things get too hairy, don't hesitate to call."

"Got you on that. But what's too hairy?"

"If things start closing in around you. Or guns."

"If someone starts waving a gun around, I'm running for the lagoon and diving in."

"Careful about that idea. This weather blowing in isn't going away any time soon."

"Hurricane Constance? I thought she was trending to the south?"

"The eye is heading straight for Oahu or Kauai. Could be a big one if it doesn't spin itself out."

"When is it supposed to hit?"

"Late tonight or early tomorrow morning. Just be careful if you take a runner during the storm."

"I think I'd rather take my chances with Constance than with anybody associated with the Swenbergs."

Honey of a Hurricane

Chapter Six

When Detective Ota stopped at the curb in front of the Swenberg house, he made it look like he was a professional driver by opening the door for her.

"Wish me luck," Maile said, while walking away. She knew better than to wave goodbye to him, but almost did anyway.

Taking only her clutch with the bare minimum necessary for the afternoon, she went up the walk to the front door. When she put a little extra motion in her hips in case someone was watching from a window, she wondered if Ota was watching from his car. The rain had stopped, at least for a while, and the sun was shining between cloudbanks. Someone must've noticed her arrive, because a young woman dressed in flowery nurses' scrubs came to the door to welcome her.

"Thanks for coming," the woman said quietly. "I'm not sure why they had someone come today."

"Why? Is there a problem?"

"No different than any other day, I guess." She stepped back to allow Maile to enter. "I'm Santos, a nurse for the man who lives here. Did anybody clue you in on the arrangement?"

Maile needed to remember she was acting the part of a hooker. That meant leaving the hat and sunglasses on, even indoors. At least that's what she assumed what a hooker would do. "I heard something from the girl that was here yesterday."

"You're not the same one? You look like the same girl. That's who they're expecting."

"She wasn't available, so I'm filling in for her."

"Dead ringer in that outfit."

Ota had been right. There was a lot more going on in the house than what anyone with the police had figured, certainly more than what Suzie had told Maile.

"She mentioned something about…" Maile stopped when she got a surprise.

A man was leaning against the corner of the wall near the entry into the vast living room, dressed in a black T-shirt and thin tan jacket. While chewing gum, he looked Maile up and down before nodding his greeting. Maile thought he was too tough to be a physical therapist or masseur for Swenberg.

"I'm not sure who I'm here for," Maile said. "Or what they're expecting. I was told it was easy entertainment, rather than my usual work."

"Know much about baseball?" the nurse asked.

"A little."

"Know what a utility player is?"

"Someone who plays any position…oh."

"That's why they were hoping for the girl that came here yesterday. You'll have a hard time topping her performance."

It was already turning out different from what Ota, or even Suzie, had told her earlier in the day. Maile needed to find a way of delaying what might turn out to be the inevitable. It might even be time to reverse course and head for the door, calling for Detective Ota to come get her.

She also needed the money Ota had promised her, and still wanted to get to the bottom of two murders related to Oscar Swenberg. If she played things right…

"Maybe I should meet the man who hired me. I heard he's in a wheelchair?"

"That's Mister Swenberg. He had an accident a while back and is still recovering."

Maile was completely out of her element, not knowing how to adlib in a situation that was completely new and different to her. "Where is he now?"

"He's in his wheelchair down by the yacht. He likes being alone while getting some sun. It's supposed to be wet again later today, so he's getting as much fresh air while he can."

Maile looked toward the back of the house, where the expansive living room passed through large sliding glass doors to a patio, with gardens and lawns beyond. A flagstone path led to the dock, where Swenberg's boat was tied up, something Maile was all too familiar with from previous visits. "I'll go see if he needs something from me."

"Soon enough. I'm supposed to show you to a guest room you can use while you're here." Nurse Santos led Maile away. "What time do you plan to leave?"

"I'm booked for four hours."

"I ask because a storm is headed this way." Santos looked at Maile to get the point across. "Supposed to hit the islands at around midnight, but the weather is supposed to turn hard later this afternoon."

"I heard. Buses don't run in heavy weather like that." It was time to adlib. With Swenberg constrained to his chair, and the masseur likely leaving soon, Maile could use the extra time to work on Oscar and Honey, wherever she was. Maile still hadn't seen her. "I should get out of here early if I can."

"Fat chance. You might get stuck here waiting out the storm."

Maile was still adlibbing. "But I have other clients later."

"Better give them a call and cancel, if that's something you guys do in your line of work."

"Not usually."

The more Santos spoke, the more Maile thought she wasn't a local Filipino, but from the mainland. She might not even be Filipino, but Mexican. "You're Mister Swenberg's private duty nurse? How long have you worked for him?"

"Just since his accident. More of a maid than a nurse. He does most of his care himself. I just lay out his things and cook meals. And make sure he takes his meds on time."

"Sometimes nursing's not very glamorous." Maile sat on the bed for a rest, hoping Santos would sit with her for a private talk. She finally took off the hat and sunglasses and set them aside. "I heard a girl lives with him?"

"That would be Honey, his girlfriend. Why are you concerned about her?"

"Is she jealous of you taking care of him?"

"She's preoccupied with other things lately."

"What's that mean?" Maile asked.

"It means she's not jealous of me, and won't be of you, if that's what you're worried about. Won't come after you with a knife, anyway."

"Probably none of my business, but you don't have a local accent," Maile said.

That's when Nurse Santos finally sat with her. "Californian. LA originally."

"What brought you to Honolulu?"

"Boyfriend, significant other, whatever they're called these days," Santos said, nonchalantly.

"You must miss him while taking care of Mister Swenberg?" Maile asked. It wasn't about Carl's murder, but she was getting some interesting gossip.

"I don't miss him as much as I thought I would've." Santos gave the impression there was more, but Maile didn't press. "You ask a lot of questions for someone in your line of work."

"Sorry. I usually don't get much chance to talk to new people."

"I try not to get too chummy with the friends and family of my clients," Santos said.

The door opened, without being knocked on first. A man came in, another tough to Maile's eyes. "What're the two of you hiding in here for?"

"Just talking," Nurse Santos said.

The thug looked back and forth between Maile and the nurse sitting on the bed. "Look, doll. You're here to work, not talk. The boss is gonna want a shave."

"He can shave his own face," Santos said.

The thug gave Santos a quick backhand. "If the boss wants the nurse to shave his face, the nurse shaves his face. And the nurse better be real careful about how she does it, understand?"

"Yeah, sure, whatever you say."

"That's right, what I say. And I say I need to check her purse."

"I don't have anything except cash and my phone," Maile said.

"Let him check." Santos touched her cheek and looked at a spot of blood on her fingertip. "He's going to anyway."

The thug took Maile's clutch and dumped the contents onto the bed. There were the usual things, a coin purse, phone, a pair of tampons rubber banded together, lipstick, a small makeup compact, and tiny flashlight. Detective Ota had given her a couple of condoms, just in case someone checked her purse. As the lipstick rolled away, he gave the flashlight a close inspection by flicking it on and off several times.

"What about the hat?" he asked.

Maile handed it over. Satisfied it wasn't a threat, he let Maile put everything back in her clutch. Once he was done with the inspection, he grabbed her phone.

"I'll hang onto this for you."

"Give me my phone!"

"Let him have it," Santos said, touching her cheek again. "There's enough trouble around here."

"You know how to shave a face?" the thug asked Maile.

"Why? Do I need one?" Maile asked in return.

"A wise guy, huh?"

"No, but from what I understand, I'm here for something else besides shaving faces."

The thug took a step back but kept his eye on the two women. "Just keep the chatter to a minimum. I don't like people chatting behind closed doors, especially a couple of dolls. Women need to learn how to shut up."

The thug left the door open when he walked out, taking a limp with him.

"Things not going so well?" Maile whispered. She took a look at the girl's face.

"Been like that ever since they got here a couple of days ago. You should've left when you had the chance."

"I might right now," Maile said. "I just need to get my phone back."

"Don't even ask for it. I think you're stuck here, now that you've seen how they are."

"How many are there?"

"The two you've met, plus three more. The one at the door is called Limps. This cheerful one is Manny, the number two guy of the group."

Neither Ota nor Suzie had said anything about these other five men in the house, but the nurse just said they'd been there for a while. Right then, it sounded like whoever was staking out the Swenberg house from the police department was falling asleep on the job, and that Suzie was a lot trickier than what Maile had given her credit for. She'd had several chances that afternoon to mention there were other men in the house than Oscar Swenberg, but never did. "Who're the rest?"

"You'll meet them soon enough."

"Apparently, they're my clients?" Maile asked.

"Only the boss, and only if he likes the look of you. He liked Suzie yesterday, though, and you're a close match."

"Maybe I'll get lucky and he won't approve of me." Maile stood and pulled Santos up to her feet. "I'll get some ice for your cheek."

"Forget it. That'll just cause more trouble."

"An ice pack?"

"Ice is reserved for drinks." Just then a door slammed somewhere in the house. "Speak of the devil, that would be Honey. She and the boss just had some private time. She'll be headed to the bar now."

Before they left the room, Santos stopped Maile and leaned in to whisper in her ear. "Whatever you do, don't drink from an open bottle. Stick to cans of soda. Some of the bottles have been spiked."

Santos raised her hand like an airline stewardess, pointing the way to the vast living room. At the back was a bar that stretched from one bedroom door to another across the width of the house. Honey was there, a drink in front of her, resting her elbows on the bar. A slender man was at the opposite end of the short bar, dressed in a mint green shirt and straw fedora. Suspenders held up his white pants. Even though his clothes were pressed and tidy, he looked just as tough as the other two Maile had seen.

"Who's this?" he asked, nodding at Maile.

"Today's guest of Mister Swenberg," Santos said. She went around to the back of the bar for a piece of ice to press on her cheek.

"What's she doing here?"

"I told you, she's a friend of Oscar."

"Don't get fresh. We didn't ask for someone today."

"Look, Mister Swenberg asked for someone to come, okay? Want me to send her away?"

"She can stay." Suspenders looked Maile up and down and allowed a smile to form on his thin lips. "Yee hee! She looks fun."

Honey of a Hurricane

Maile gulped, but did her best to hide how she was reacting internally. When she drew near the bar, she heard what sounded like a horse race being called by an announcer, odd since there was no horse racing in Hawaii, or legal gambling.

"If you'd like a drink, have a seat," Santos said before she left Maile to go outside. "Nobody'll bother you."

Chapter Seven

Maile smelled Honey's body odor mixed with perfume before she even got to her. Maile had been an athlete for most of her life and was accustomed to other people's sweaty smells, and when used lightly, patchouli wasn't bad. That day, though, the combination was a little too potent.

Honey looked up from her phone screen, which was where the horse race was being shown. She was underclad in a leather miniskirt, and her top was also leather, but instead of buttons holding it closed, chains allowed for freedom of movement for whatever was hidden beneath. From what Maile saw, not only was there a lot of movement going on, but plenty of cleavage. Honey's smile was as fake as everything else about her.

"You were here yesterday, right?" she said with a voice thick with liquor. She'd either been hitting the sauce heavily all day or had a bee sting on her tongue. "I called for the same girl to come back."

"That's the message I got," Maile said. So far, Honey wasn't recognizing her, assuming she was Suzie, about the only thing going in Maile's favor right then. She'd been there for half an hour and was already looking for a way out.

"I remember the outfit. Looks good on you."

"Thanks. I wear it a lot." Maile wondered if that's what prostitutes normally talked about.

There were three bar stools to choose from, and Maile took the one in the middle, splitting the difference in distance between Honey and the man in the suspenders. Another man in a tent-like white pullover stepped out from around the corner.

"Just some iced tea or coffee," Maile said. That's when she remembered Santos' admonition about sticking to canned sodas. "Make it a ginger ale. A can, if you have it."

Before getting the drink, the bartender nodded to the man in the suspenders.

"Need to check you first," Suspenders said.

"For?" Maile asked. She knew she had nothing incriminating or worthy of confiscation. She didn't even have pockets in her outfit, but needed to play the game. "The other guy already looked in my purse."

"Just give her a drink," Honey said, not looking up from the race on her phone screen.

"Need to frisk her."

"I said, give her a drink!"

The bartender went about the task of getting a can of ginger ale from the fridge and poured it into a glass.

"Something with a little spirit to it," Honey demanded. "No reason for me to drink alone."

The bartender held up bottles of vodka and rum, but Maile waved them off. She watched carefully as two lumps of ice were dropped into her glass.

"Thanks," Maile said, more to Honey than the bartender.

The first thug Maile had met, the one at the front door and in the bedroom, swaggered up to her. "Gonna get frisked, one way or another."

"Just let him," Honey muttered. "Get it over with."

Maile slowly stood. "I don't have anything you need to worry about."

"Yee hee!" Suspenders said. "There's more to broads to worry about than guns."

The thug with the limp spent most of his time checking Maile's hips for a hidden holster, his hands under her tiny skirt. Finding nothing, he turned his hands and attention to her chest.

"I don't have anything in my bra."

"Looking for a wire." He turned her around and pushed a hand beneath her top. With another feel inside, he was done.

"Satisfied?" Maile asked, adjusting her clothes.

"Never," Limps said, walking away.

"Yee hee! Either am I!" Suspenders said.

"Why don't you shut up and find something useful to do," Honey said, now watching a new horse race on her phone.

The whole scene was beyond odd to Maile. Honey was plastered and watching horse races, Oscar Swenberg was outside in the rain enjoying the fresh air, and his nurse didn't mind at all getting slapped. One of the men wore suspenders and had a facial tic, and the man who groped her needed a manicure. They looked and acted like gangsters from an old black and white movie. There was a lot more going on in the house that day than what she signed up for. At least the men hadn't figured out she was a different girl from the day before. Or maybe they just didn't care.

Not knowing what else to do, Maile struck up a conversation with Honey.

"You like horse racing?"

"Not really."

"Why are you watching?"

"I used to go watch live racing. Ever been to the horse races in LA?"

"Never been to LA."

"These are live races that I can wager on. I'm not supposed to have this app in Hawaii, but I don't care. I don't wager real money." Honey urged on her horse down the stretch. "Come on, Lady Venus! Come on!"

Maile tried watching what was playing on the screen, but having never seen a horse race before, she didn't understand what was happening. Her horse must've won when Honey slapped the bar with a hand and cheered. She pushed her empty drink glass toward the bartender, who began washing it.

"Fill it," she said.

"You've had enough."

"What?"

"Bar's closed."

"Who says?"

"The boss says."

"The boss just told me I can have a drink."

"Yeah, that's right. One drink and then you're done."

"But you watered it down!"

"You're done drinkin'."

Maile felt sorry for the girl, that it sounded like a frequent refrain from the bartender to refuse another pour. But it was barely mid-afternoon, so her heart didn't break too much over Honey having to dry out for a while.

She left her ginger ale alone and scanned the large living room. At the far end were large sliding glass doors that went outside. Beyond, she saw Oscar in his wheelchair out at the dock, pointing and waving his one good arm around, having his nurse do things with the yacht's ropes.

"Mind if I go say hello to Oscar?" she asked.

"Help yourself. Nothing in here to do," Honey said, watching another batch of horses load into a starting gate. That's when someone came out of the bedroom near the bar. With only a glimpse, Maile saw the room was large, probably the master bedroom. This guy was thick through the middle, and the best dressed of everyone. He nodded a greeting to the other two men.

"Who's that?" he asked, referring to Maile.

"Company. She's okay, so far," Suspenders said.

"Where's the nurse?"

"Outside with the cripple."

"Get her in here. The boss wants a shave."

"Think that's a good idea?"

"I think it'd be a bad idea for her to get smart about it. Go get her."

Limps went out to get the nurse, and brought her back with one of her arms locked in his grip.

"Not here to take care of your boss," she griped, once they were inside.

"You have a new client. All he wants is a shave. I know you know how to do that because I see you shave the cripple every morning."

That meant to Maile the group of men had been in the house for at least a couple of days. They treated Honey differently from the nurse. Honey was tolerated as if she had some sort of value; the nurse wasn't anything more than a service provider. That started a whole new set of qualms for Maile, making her wonder what her role was as the third woman in the mix.

When Santos went into the bedroom, the other men followed her.

"Both of you, also," Suspenders said, looking at Maile and Honey.

"Why?" Maile asked. She had concocted the plan of taking a runner through neighbors' backyards once she was outside. If she had to, she dive into the boat channel and swim for safety. She figured contending with yachts and cabin cruisers was a better bet than what the next few hours held for her in the house. "I'm just going to say hello to my host."

"Your host is waiting for a shave," Limps said.

"Easier if we just go in," Honey said, slipping off her stool and finding her sea legs.

Inside the bedroom, a skinny man was dressed in a bathrobe. He was facing away. When Honey took a seat on the foot end of the unmade bed, she patted the space next to her for Maile to sit. Santos made it look like she knew her way around the bathroom, and returned with a can of shaving cream and a safety razor.

"Not with that," the boss said. "Use the things from my kit."

His voice was familiar to Maile, but she wasn't sure why.

The nurse brought out a leather grooming kit. "I don't know how to use a straight razor," she said, unfolding the thing in her hand.

"Better learn in a hurry." Two of his thugs were positioned on either side of him, leaning against dressers or cabinets. Two others had gone to keep an eye on

Oscar outside, leaving the bartender to watch from the doorway. When the boss sat in a chair in the middle of the room, Maile got her next surprise of the day when she saw his face reflected in the mirror.

An ungodly puckering sensation swept through her body when she realized who the boss was. She did her best to sit still and not hide her face with a hand.

Limps got up close and personal with Nurse Santos. "Make sure you don't accidently let that blade slip."

"It won't slip," Santos said. "I've just never used a razor like this before."

Suspenders pushed a pistol muzzle into the nurse's ribs. "It's not going to slip, right?"

"No, it won't slip."

"What happens if it does?"

"I…"

"I'll tell you what happens. Blood for blood, that's what happens," he told her.

"Is that really necessary?" Maile asked.

Keeping the pistol stuck in the nurse's ribs, Suspenders looked at Maile. "You want to take her place, doll?"

Maile's mind swirled with ambitious confusion, wondering how to respond. Saving her was Honey's gentle pat to her thigh. "It's easier for everybody if these guys make all the decisions."

"Shaving men is not what I'm good at," was all Maile could think to say. She put her eyes back on the skinny man in the chair.

Only a few feet away sat Lenny the snitch, waiting for a shave. Somehow, he'd transformed from infamous police informant to some sort of gangster boss, handing out orders to lackeys at his disposal.

Santos laid a towel over Lenny's chest and wrapped a hot, wet towel over his face. She was able to make a lather of soap in a ceramic cup with a brush, like an old-fashioned barber would do. The process would've been interesting for Maile to watch, but she had some thinking to do.

What she couldn't remember is if she and Lenny had ever met in person. She'd seen him a few times at the police station downtown, when he was providing information to the police in return for a payment under the table. What she didn't know was if he had ever seen her there, and if he would recognize her. With each passing moment in the house, the walls of her world were closing in around her.

It was time to pull the ejection lever, but she didn't have her phone to call Ota. As fit as she was, she could out-run anyone in the house. But not a bullet. Suspenders had a gun, which gave him the upper hand in any situation. She had to assume that they all had guns, and acting as tough as they were, wouldn't be afraid to use them. The nurse had been smacked in the chops for no good reason, and Honey was being emotionally muscled through forced abstinence after a roll in the sack with the boss. Swenberg, the owner of the house and the reason Maile was there that day, was sitting alone in his wheelchair in the rain staring at his yacht. But it was the guy in the chair, Lenny the snitch, that was calling all the shots.

Santos took off the towel and began smearing the thin lather on Lenny's face with her fingertips.

"Who's that in the yellow shirt and big hair?" Lenny asked.

"Showed up a little while ago," Portly said. Apparently his real name was Manny. "Want me to get rid of her?"

"Where'd she come from?"

"She's my friend, okay?" Honey said. She'd moved on from horse races to playing video poker on her phone.

"You called her?"

"Oscar wanted the same girl that was here yesterday."

That answered Maile's question about the clothes. She was wearing the same outfit that Suzie had worn. As far as she could tell, she had Honey fooled into believing she was Suzie, even if Santos had spotted her. For whatever reason, none of the men seemed to care who she was.

"How many more are coming?" Lenny asked.

"No more. I'm sorry, okay? I forgot you didn't want any more girls."

Maile wasn't sure what was going on right then, but she was glad she wasn't being 'got rid of' by a thug, whatever that might mean.

"By the way, my name's…"

"Keep quiet," Suspenders said.

"Better do as he says," Lenny said. "Braces has got a temper."

'And a gun,' Maile thought. She watched as Santos took the first swipe at Lenny's face with the straight razor. The edge slid down his cheek, removing whatever stubble was there. When no blood rose, it was so far, so good.

"Maybe I should go?" Maile offered as politely as possible.

"You're staying put. As long as we're here, you're here, and so is everyone else."

"How much longer is that gonna be?" Honey asked.

"Anybody hear from Mickey?" Lenny asked as Santos slid the razor down his other cheek.

"Haven't heard nothing."

"Manny, get Mickey on the phone."

Manny, the portly one and assistant director of the drama that was being performed, went to a corner to make the call.

Maile watched intently as the nurse shaved Lenny's face. She worked slowly, methodically, while Lenny talked. Mostly about Mickey, whoever that was. When she finished with his cheeks, Santos put her attention on his neck, holding his head back with one hand while working with the razor with the other. Maile wondered if she would be as disciplined as Santos if she were the one wielding the razor right then.

"Be extra careful, understand?" Limps got in the nurse's ear, once again pressing the muzzle of his gun into her ribs. "Blood for blood, and I decide how much."

Nurse Santos went to work on Lenny's neck with the straight razor.

"You think I don't recognize you, don't you, doll face?" Lenny said, after the first slow swipe of the blade.

Maile knew it had to mean her. "Me?"

Lenny turned around in his chair to face Maile, forcing Santos to pull the razor away quickly. "Yeah, you. You're working for the cops."

"The cops? No. I'm here because Honey told me to come back today. I didn't mean to interrupt your party."

Lenny eased back for Santos to start again. "Not having a party. Just conducting a little business."

"Didn't mean to interrupt that, either."

"Well, you have. Now I have to figure out what to do with you."

By now, Santos was almost done with her project, and Honey's attention was on the conversation instead of her phone.

"You don't have to do anything with me," Maile said. "Just let me leave."

"To go to Ota, you mean?" Lenny pushed Santos' hands away and took a towel from her to wipe his face. "Enough of that."

"I don't know who Ota is."

Lenny went to the mirror, still wiping his face. There was a nick along a jawline he was trying to stop from bleeding. "He's the detective you've met at the station. I've seen you at his desk."

"I think that's his name. Yeah, sure, he's picked me up a couple of times. Doesn't mean I'm working with him."

"You broads think you're smart. Well, you're not. You're up to something, and before tonight is out, I'll know what it is."

"Boss," Manny said, coming back with the phone in his hand. "Mickey said not till the morning."

"What? Gimme that phone." Lenny put the phone up to his ear, still trying to stop the bleeding on his jaw. "Mickey? What's wrong?"

Maile watched as Lenny listened for a reply, and tried to guess what was being discussed.

"Storm? What storm?"

As if on cue, wind hit the house.

"I don't care about any hurricane. Look, I made deals during earthquakes and forest fires. Some rain's not going to stop me."

Lenny listened for a moment.

"Forget that. Either you get here by midnight or the deal is off, understand?"

Lenny tossed the phone back to Manny to end the call. "Higgs, set out my gray suit."

"Which shirt, boss?" the bartender asked.

"The blue one, of course."

Dabbing at his jaw again, Lenny called Santos over. "Look at this blood, nurse. You got a way of making it stop?"

"It's not so much."

From what she could see from where Maile sat, she agreed. It was barely a speck of red.

Lenny leaned in close to Santos' ear to whisper. It almost looked as though her dark complexion was turning pale as she listened.

"Yes, sir, I understand."

"The rest of you get out," Lenny said, turning around to take off his robe.

Honey broke for the door, and Maile wasn't far behind, followed by Manny and Higgs.

80

Chapter Eight

Santos almost ran from the room when she was done with the shave, and bolted for outside, going straight to the yacht to check on Swenberg. When Honey stopped at the bar to coerce a drink from Higgs, Maile continued through the house, now aiming for the yacht to greet Oscar. She'd got nothing out of Santos about Carl's murder, and Honey was in no shape to carry on an intelligible conversation, so it was time to go straight to the source. One way or another, she was taking her mind off the thugs in the house right then.

"Where you goin', girlie?" Manny asked, following along behind her.

"Just out to see Mister Swenberg."

"Just don't get any clever ideas about taking a swim."

"Or what?"

He opened his jacket to reveal a holstered pistol.

"I'm not going anywhere. If I did try to leave, it wouldn't be swimming, not in this weather." She was serious about that, too. The water in the channel had turned to chop, impossible to swim except for the hardiest of athletes.

Manny leaned up against a wall and lit a cigarette while keeping watch on Maile. Most of the back wall of the house was made up of open doors, creating an indoor/outdoor feel. The coming storm was being heralded by gusts of moist wind blowing into the house.

Maile remembered the long flagstone walkway that led to the yacht dock on the channel. The closer she got to the boat, the slower she walked, thinking of the time she snuck onto the property in the middle of the night, just to snoop for evidence of murder in Oscar's two half-brothers' deaths. The only person that ever knew about that moment was Detective Ota, and he hadn't been upset enough to lock her in a cell. Here she was today, trapped at the Swenberg house, in the custody of gangsters.

The smell of the seawater was heavy in the air, and waves were splashing against docks. Some of the more expensive boats were being taken out to open water to wait out the storm. She watched Santos jump aboard The Mongoose, the Swenberg yacht, while Oscar watched.

There was a second boat moored at Swenberg's dock, this one a charter fishing boat, with long poles extending out to either side as outriggers. Its white hull gleamed in the broken sunlight, making it look brand new. Maybe it was a rental that had been reserved by the gangsters, but it seemed a shame it was tied to a dock instead of being used. Even a simple tour of that part of the island would be better than sitting in the house, begging for booze or watching while a turncoat had his face shaved.

Something niggled at Maile's mind as she thought of Honey begging for booze but not getting much, and how stoned she was anyway. Even Suzie had mentioned something...what was it again? Maile couldn't quite put her finger on what was bothering her so much right then.

Before she got to Oscar, Maile adjusted the fit of her top and skirt. He was in a wheelchair, but he was still a man. There might be many ways to a man's heart; Maile needed to find a way to get to his soul for a few answers about murder. If she had to use a little cheesecake to do it, fine with her. She wanted to find the murderer of Oscar's two half-brothers as much as Detective Ota did.

When she got to him, Maile looked at the neighbors' property and wondered if she could outrun a bullet from that distance. There were walls and tress to hide behind, and she'd have to race through several gardens before she found a way to the street. Even then, one of the thugs would be in a car out looking for her. She also had no way of contacting Ota without her phone.

Then there was the dreadful idea of abandoning Honey and Nurse Santos with a gang of thugs. Maile was even feeling a little soft-hearted for Oscan Swenberg right then.

With the likelihood of escape being minimal, and the notion of leaving behind innocent others, Maile decided to stick to Ota's little program for a little while longer.

"Hello, Mister Swenberg. Nice to see you again."

Both of his legs were in casts that reached to his hips, and one arm was in a bulky sling. There was a healing cut on one cheekbone.

He barely looked at her. "Suzie, isn't it?"

That question was answered. He recognized her as being the hooker from the day before, not as Mary Spellman from a party a few weeks before. Detective Ota and the stakeout were proving to be completely oblivious to what was happening at the Swenberg house. It also answered why the men in the house were staying there, rather than coming outside. "Yes, thank you for remembering. How are you feeling?"

"I've been better." He watched as his nurse tied a knot in a line that secured the yacht to a cleat on the dock. It looked like Santos knew as much about boats as Maile did. "Not like that! I told you to make overlapping figure-eights on the cleat."

"Is your nurse taking good care of you?" Maile asked.

"Taking better care of me than she is of my yacht." He tried pushing forward in his wheelchair but didn't get far using only one hand. "We have some weather blowing in. I need that thing secure so it doesn't tip."

"I doubt they have many boatmanship courses in nursing school. Want me to get one of those guys from the house to help her? It looks like a hard job for just one person."

"They have their own boat to worry about, and so far, none of them have been out here working on it. If they think I'm going to, they can forget it."

A man wearing a yacht captain's hat came from the cabin on the fishing boat. He was Polynesian of some sort. The hat looked out of place on his head with the T-shirt and shorts he was wearing. "Someone need help?"

"Can you show her what to do?" Oscar said, pointing at the nurse, still trying to figure out which line went to which cleat, and what to do with them.

"Is there something I can help with?" Maile asked.

"You're here for decoration and someone intelligent to talk to," Oscar said.

Maile almost laughed that Suzie would've been considered an intelligent conversationalist. Decorative figure, yes; stimulating chatter, not so much.

The fishing boat skipper went to work, showing Santos which ropes went to their proper cleats and how to tie the knots. Looking satisfied, Oscar asked Maile to push him back to the house, via a trip along the garden path. The steady afternoon breeze that made up the usual tradewinds was already turning blustery, with dark clouds crowding the horizon in every direction. The leading edge of the storm was looming.

"Suzie, do you know why you've been invited back today?"

There was a question Ota or Suzie hadn't prepped her for. She was still trying to pass herself off as an Asian hooker. So far, she hadn't been propositioned yet since getting to the house two hours before. "Not really sure, actually. Your friend Honey said you wanted the same girl as yesterday to come back. The men in the house were a little surprised that I came back, though. I'm not sure why."

"Your name isn't Suzie, is it?"

Uh oh. He knew she was masquerading. "Um, well, no."

"You're not Mary Spellman either, are you? Isn't that the name you gave me a while back at the party?"

"Yes, I suppose it was."

"I thought so. You gave me some sort of song and dance about being a wealthy widow in Kahala. I checked your name out, and guess what I found?"

"Nothing?"

"Right. Even Honey had her suspicions that day. You're Maile Spencer, a tour guide, right?"

"How did you know that?"

"You were on the TV news a while back in a story about my brother's death. Your face was on TV, anyway. Right after that, you showed up here at my house."

"I didn't know the news people shared my name. I tried to keep that out of it."

"They didn't mention it. Honey figured it out." They stopped at a small intimate area, a tiny private niche in the lush plantings. "Honey's not the brightest bulb in the chandelier, but when it comes to remembering faces and physiques, she's unbeatable. Show her a picture of any celebrity, entertainer, or athlete's body, and nine times out of ten, she'll be spot on at knowing who it is. Social life, net worth, latest gossip, everything." Oscar shook his head. "Ask her to add two numbers together, and nine times out of ten, she'll be clueless. Don't bother giving her a calculator. Flying a space shuttle would be easier for her than using a Casio."

"How'd she recognize me?" Maile asked.

"You were a year older than her in high school, yes? And a cheerleader? She apparently took your spot on the cheer squad after you graduated."

"Back then, I was very light in weight and athletic, which meant I was the girl they'd toss to the top of the human pyramid. I remember she was built the same."

"She's quite pleased to show off the pictures from back then. You're in a few."

"I'm still trying to keep mine hidden." Maile had some damage control to do, if she wanted to stay out of even more trouble. As it was, she doubted she'd get much out of Oscar because of her deceit that he'd discovered. That would likely make him suspicious of any questions she might ask. "I'm very sorry about deceiving you like that a few weeks ago. It's just that I was asked to be the date of someone invited to your party, and was afraid that if I used my real name, Honey wouldn't want me there. I'm not really your kind of people."

He waved his hand dismissively. "Forget about it. This is my house, not hers or anyone else's. Much to their concern, I make the final decision on what happens here, no one else."

"But you were expecting Suzie to come back today, not me to show up."

"That was a surprise, especially when she said she was going to be busy today with her clients. I wasn't sure of who to expect, but here you are again. Apparently, you don't have any tours to give, or any clients to see."

Did that mean he thought Maile was not just a tour guide, but also a prostitute? This was getting complicated with too many details for Maile to remember. "I don't know if she's busy or not. She asked me to cover for her and offered this job to me."

"Easy job for you today, I guess."

"I'm still not sure who my client is, or what's expected of me?" she asked.

"In the last few days, the other girls were brought in for that Lenny character in there, along with Honey. He didn't want anyone today because those clowns are supposedly pulling out later. But he had his ways with Honey today anyway."

"But she was the one who called Suzie, right?" Maile asked.

"She was hoping that if Suzie came back, Lenny would want her and leave Honey alone. I tried telling her to forget it, but she didn't listen. Somehow, she was able to get to a phone and make the call without them noticing." He laughed, but without mirth. "If she had half a brain in her think skull, she would've called the cops."

"Lenny and his guys don't seem to be the types that like to be crossed. Why are they here?" she asked.

"Best you don't know about that," Oscar said. "But if that jerk hasn't taken you into the bedroom by now, I doubt he will. He has other things on his mind today."

The home invasion by the gangsters seemed personal to Oscar. Maile also wondered if he and Honey were on the outs for some other reason, or if it was because of Lenny putting her to his personal use. With the way Honey was staying inside gambling on her phone, and Oscar outside directing maintenance of his yacht from a wheelchair, maybe they had a bigger storm in their lives right then than what was looming on the horizon. That's when Maile noticed the black clouds that were now overhead, the breeze having turned to steady wind as they talked.

Maile needed to get that phone from Honey, and without being seen by the thugs. She couldn't think of Ota's private number, but a call to 9-1-1 would be good enough. Even calling Suzie to let her know things had gone south at the house, and to let Ota know it was time to bail them out might work.

"Maybe Honey can call the police with her phone?" Maile whispered.

Oscar shook his head. "Not her phone. Not even a real phone or connected to cellular or data. Just a toy for her to play with."

"How'd she call Suzie to have her come back today?"

"Snuck into the bathroom while Lenny was showering and used his. When he discovered that, he put her to work in the bedroom to pay for her crime. From what I heard, neither one of them were having much fun. That's when I came out here."

"I wish I could think of a way to get use out of here," Maile said.

"I doubt those idiots inside would let you get far. If anyone tries anything, they'll be leaving on a morgue stretcher. I do have a few questions for you, though."

"About your brother?"

"Yes, Frank, the younger of my half-brothers. The news reporters said you were the one who found his body on Diamond Head?"

"Yes." Now she was getting somewhere, with Oscar bringing up the subject on his own. Maile was in fact one of two people who found the murdered body of Frank Swenberg at the summit of Diamond Head, but she wasn't telling him the identity of the other person. "Pretty bad taste on my part to come to a party at your house only days after his death."

"Pretty bad form on my part to hold that party. I'd only learned of his death that morning, and decided to have the party anyway. But we weren't close. News of his passing felt about the same as learning about the death of a neighbor from my childhood. It was like, 'Oh, well, that's too bad.' Then it was time to move on. He's been trouble ever since."

Finally, Maile was getting something Detective Ota might want to know. "I heard the police arrested you for it."

He nodded. "Kept me there overnight, tried to sweat me. I think they have no leads and were getting desperate for an arrest."

"Seems like the police are like that sometimes. Do you have any idea who might've done that to him?"

"Stabbed him in the eyeball? I could only guess, and when I offered my hunches to the police, they weren't humored. They think I know more than what I'm letting on."

"That's something else the police are always convinced of, right from the beginning of any investigation, that we all know more than what we're telling them."

Oscar looked up at her. "How do you know that?"

She'd just slipped up and almost showed her hand of cards. "Oh, just from watching TV, I guess." A few raindrops hit Maile. If her face got wet, her heavy makeup would smear, risking exposing her identity to Honey. If she blabbed in front of Lenny, Maile's goose would be cooked. "Maybe we should get inside before we get wet."

"I don't mind a few raindrops. Once we go in, we're stuck with the others until the storm passes." He nodded in the direction of the house. "And that's a group you don't want to be stuck with."

It was time to push an agenda. "I've been wondering about Frank's murder. You have no idea who was so mad at him that they wanted him dead?"

"You're starting sound like a cop again."

"Sorry." She had pushed her agenda too hard. "Who are these guys?"

"Have you met all of them?"

"I think so. Some tough looking guy with a limp that follows me around, a skinny guy wearing suspenders who laughs a lot, a bartender that won't pour drinks, and someone named Manny, who takes care of the boss."

"They're the bodyguards. There's a fifth that spends most of his time in the master bedroom suite."

"Yes, Lenny. The rest of us watched while Santos gave him a shave. Do you know much about him?" she asked.

"Apparently, an old business associate of my brothers from the mainland."

"What's his real name?"

"Leonard Gallo, a brother in the once powerful Gallo crime family in LA. Do you know him?"

When the chips were down, Maile could lie as well as the best of them. This time, she was stumped for an answer. "Why would I know someone like that? I'm just a tour guide."

"And a hooker. Seems he knows most of you girls in Honolulu." Oscar tried scratching an itch through the cast on a leg, accomplishing nothing but more frustration. "He's getting on my nerves."

Santos came out with umbrellas for them to use, and ran back into the house again. Maile knew by then her hairdo was glued together from all the spray she'd used and the moisture in the air. Even her sheer silk scarf was stuck down to her neck.

"I don't understand why he's still here if you don't want him in your house?"

"Not much choice."

"Why not? Just tell him and his friends to clear out."

"No so easy." He used his back scratcher stick to whack one of his casts. "I've already tried that and didn't get far."

"You mean…"

"Yeah. Braces, that's the guy with the stupid suspenders, worked on my shoulder, while the other two used a sledge hammer on my knees. So, pardon me if I don't stand up and fight for myself right now."

"Sorry. Lenny told them to do that to you?"

"He sat in a chair and watched. At least until I started to make too much noise, and he told them to knock it off. He went back to bed and Honey took me to the hospital."

"She didn't call for an ambulance?"

"When gangsters give you a beating, you don't call for an ambulance. Somebody puts you in the back seat of their car and drives you to the ER."

"But why'd you come back if you knew these guys were here?" she asked.

"Lenny sent Manny along. He even paid the bill. When someone like Lenny or Manny opens his pocketbook while holding a gun to your ribs, you do whatever he wants you to."

"They didn't hurt her?" Maile asked. She wasn't sure why she cared about Honey all of a sudden.

"She's valuable to them. But Lenny doesn't like drunks, so there's this constant game of her trying to get too drunk for him to want her, but not so drunk she gets beat up for it." He nodded his head toward the house. "They cut off the booze at noon, and by mid-afternoon, she's sober enough for Lenny. When Honey or the hooker goes in the bedroom with Lenny, I come out here. They think it's for the fresh air and sunshine. I just don't want to hear them going at it in my bedroom. Or used to be my bedroom. Not that this place will be mine for much longer." He pretended to wipe raindrops from his face, but Maile could tell he was wiping away tears.

"They're making you sell it?"

"I owe money to them. Or others just like them. I can thank Honey and my brothers for that."

Oscar had inadvertently steered himself back to why Ota had Maile in the house. "They owed money and you're paying it back?"

"Honey went into heavy debt, and got bailed out a couple of times. Unfortunately, that was by high-roller loan sharks. She's found a way of paying off that debt, and bless her heart, without asking me for money. But when I tried selling this place to get the money to pay off her debts, it wasn't nearly enough. I couldn't come up with enough money quick enough to get her out of the trouble she's in."

"You said something about your brothers being a part of it?"

"They're the lucky ones." Oscar turned his wheelchair to go back inside the house now that rain was falling in earnest. "They're dead."

Maile wasn't sure if it was alarm or a feeling of being demoralized that was settling in. "Sorry for all your trouble, and I hate to abandon you, but is there a way I can get out of this mess?"

"Probably not without suffering broken bones. There's something you don't know."

"What's that?"

"Lenny and the others know who you are. It was no accident that you're here today rather than the one that was here yesterday."

"How'd he..." More confusion. "How'd Lenny accomplish that? Because Suzie traded with me only this afternoon, not long before I got here."

"Lenny knows a lot of people in town. In a lot of towns, actually."

"But why me? Is Lenny thinking I'm going to provide some favors when Honey needs a break?"

He waved his hand at her. "Anyone can come here for that."

"What, then?"

"Somehow he learned you're the one that found Frank's body at Diamond Head and wanted you here. Why, I don't know. All I know is that we're getting wet and there's too much wind."

It was nearly dark when Maile pushed Oscar toward the house. Most of the sliding doors had been closed and the louvered blinds drawn. Rainwater was pouring from the tiled roof in tiny cascades. She almost would rather have remained outside on the patio than go in with the others. As it was, she could start running and they'd never know she was missing until she was back to the transit center. But her bag, along with her bus pass and phone, were in the house under the watchful eye of Suspenders, officially known as Braces.

Maile had one last question before they got back inside. "I'm still not sure why Lenny is playing house in your home?"

"Have you heard them talk about someone named Mickey?"

"Yes. They made a phone call to him. Who's that?"

"The final player in the game. When Mickey gets here, it'll all become quite clear."

Neither Maile nor Oscar cared about the rainwater that dripped off his chair onto the hardwood floor as she pushed him through the living room.

"How's the weather?" Higgs, the bartender, asked. All of them were clustered around the bar.

"Wet. Where's Honey?" Oscar asked.

"Have a seat, pal," Limps said. He looked on edge about something, tapping a swizzle stick on the bar. His tongue was working an olive pick from one side of his mouth to the other.

"Maybe you haven't noticed, but I already am seated. Where's Honey?"

"In with the boss," Braces said, laughing.

Oscar turned his wheelchair so he looked away back toward the ocean.

Maile sat at the bar on the same stool Honey had used earlier. "May I have my phone, please?"

"No," Braces said. He laughed for no reason that Maile could see. "I'll give you something else, though."

"No, you won't."

Braces moved to the stool next to Maile's. "Come on, doll. Let's have some fun."

"Knock it off," Manny said from the corner of the room.

"Not talkin' to you."

"The boss said no more funny business until this job is done," Manny chirped back.

"That's with Honey. He never said hands off this one." Braces reached for Maile's arm, but she tugged it away.

"You wouldn't like me," Maile growled.

"Why not?"

"Not your type."

"You got the right kind of figure. That's my type, doll."

Maile was just about to take a swing at his face, when the master bedroom door opened. Honey came out, her hair disheveled, hooking the chains together to close her top again. When she looked up, it was at Oscar. She went to him, touching his good shoulder when she got there.

He shrugged her off.

With that, Honey went to the bar and sat next to Maile, opposite from Braces.

"Pour me," she told Higgs.

"Bar's closed," Braces said.

Higgs shrugged and turned away when Honey looked at him with begging eyes.

"Just want a drink!"

When Honey was still ignored, Maile raised her voice. "Give her a drink."

Maile was also ignored.

Honey made her way around to the back of the bar and poured a shot for herself. Before she could take a drink, Braces pried the glass from her hand and tossed the whiskey out, before setting the glass upside-down on the bar.

"Why...what's that for?" Honey muttered.

"The boss says, the bar's closed."

Honey left the bar and fell into an easy chair in the living room, whimpering. "Just wanted a drink."

The bedroom door opened again, only partway. Light from inside the room spilled out across the floor, past the bar. A shadow passed through, the outline of a man walking, pacing, inside the room. While the others ignored it, Maile watched.

Maybe Lenny would be in a better mood now that he'd had some afternoon exercise. Maybe he'd be cranky with the coming of the storm. Maybe whoever Mickey was would show up soon and the ordeal would end. But Maile had the idea that things weren't drawing to a close soon, or in a way she could manage.

The door opened a little more. The man's shadow filled the light on the floor. When a hard gust of wind hit the house, rafters creaked and a draft pushed the door closed.

The door opened, more forcefully. The man stepped out and leaned against the bar. "Is this the storm?"

Maile looked at him, stared at Lenny, trying to guess what was in his mind right then.

"The start of it," said Oscar.

"Who's asking you?" Lenny said.

Braces laughed. "Yee hee! No one!"

Honey of a Hurricane

Honey turned around in her easy chair with a little girl's apologetic look to her face. "Lenny, may I have a drink?"

"Bar's closed. Nothing for you after twelve noon. You know that."

"Lenny, please..."

Lenny took the glass of water Higgs had poured. "Stupid lush. All you've done for the last three days is look for the bottom of a bottle. Great Caribbean adventure, searching for treasure at the bottom of a bottle of rum." He laughed at her. "Well, guess what? This ain't the Caribbean, and adventures with you are getting boring."

"Just one. Please, Lenny."

They stood in silence as the storm grew outside. Palm fronds swatted against the side of the house, rain pattered on windowpanes. Maile watched Honey and Oscar. The storm must've been getting to the girl, her hands shaking so hard, nerves ready to crack. Maile's nerves weren't in such good shape right then, either.

"How come you don't have shutters?" Lenny asked no one in particular. "Must've spent a lot on building this place. It should have shutters on the windows."

When Honey began to whimper again, Oscar turned his wheelchair around to face Lenny. "Pour her a drink."

Lenny continued walking through the room, looking at it as if it was for the first time. "These are the tropics. You get storms here. A place like this ought to have shutters on the windows."

Lenny turned around before he got to the glass sliding doors. He stood to watch for a moment, and when a hard gust hit the house, he stepped back. When another gust pummeled the house, he went back toward Honey.

"All these windows and no shutters. The noise. One of those palm trees could come through any minute. I bet one will by the end of the night." He stopped walking when he was next to where Honey was crying. "What do you think, Manny? Think one of these palms will come through a window?"

"Could be, boss."

"What about you, Higgs?"

"Never seen a blow like this one," the bartender answered. He wasn't in much better shape than Honey, when it came to watching the windows and ceiling.

"Yee hee! I think the whole roof's coming off!" said Braces.

Lenny nudged Honey. "What about you? You have any deep thoughts about it?"

"About the storm?"

"No, about nuclear Armageddon and the end of the world?" Lenny laughed as loudly as his gangster friends did.

Honey put her head down again. "Just wanna drink. Is there something wrong with that?"

Lenny leaned down to her. "All you want's a drink? Why didn't you say so? Higgs, pour her a long one."

Everyone in the room watched as Higgs filled a glass. When Honey started for the bar, Lenny got in her way.

"Gonna have to earn it."

"She's done enough to earn whatever she wants," Oscar said.

Honey of a Hurricane

"Quiet, cripple. You still have one good arm. It doesn't have to stay that way."

Oscar turned his wheelchair around again to face away. Seeing that, Santos left her perch on the couch and went to sit with him.

"If you won't give her a drink, you can at least leave her alone," Maile said.

"Quiet. I have enough trouble with women. I don't need you making more."

Maile did her best to look tough when she glared at him.

"Maybe you want to take her place?" he asked.

"I'm not here for you."

Lenny walked to a halfway point between Maile and Honey. "You have a lot of smart answers. Let me ask you a question. Think our little entertainer should have a drink?"

"I think she's earned one."

"That doesn't answer my question. I asked if she should have one."

Maile moved the glass of liquor to the front of the bar. "It's been poured. Why not let her have it?"

Lenny's smile started to fade. He glanced at the drink. "She can have it as soon as she earns it."

"Doing what?" Maile asked. "She just did a performance for you in the bedroom. What else do you want?"

The wind got heavier, with more bashing of branches and fronds against the house. Rain was blowing in sideways under the deep patio eaves, hitting the sliding glass doors. In spite of the storm, inside the house was hot and stuffy, a sweat growing on their faces.

Maile felt a small stream leave her hairline and run down the back of her neck. Her Tabu scent kicked in.

Lenny was looking at Honey again. "I think we all need to be entertained. What about that little tease you did for me the other night? I bet the others would like to see it." He turned around to look at Maile. "Unless you'd like to? Last chance."

Maile swallowed, wondering all over again how she got roped into doing this job for Ota, someone she was liking less with each passing hour. She still didn't think much of Honey, but she felt sorry for her now that she saw the simple girl hiding beneath the luxury façade.

She pushed the drink glass to the edge of the bar. "Let her have her drink."

"Soon enough," Lenny said. "What do you do? For work, I mean. You look too classy to work the streets."

Everyone in the room looked at Maile waiting for her response, except Oscar, whose head was hanging down. To Maile, there was no good answer right then.

"I'm a tour guide."

Lenny laughed while Braces yee-hee'd. "You mean with a little flag and bullhorn at Waikiki?"

"Maybe."

"Leave her alone," moaned Honey. "She's got nothing to do with you."

"Do much dancing for those dollar tips, Tour Guide?"

"Take one of my tours and you can find out."

"Oh, you really do have all the answers!" Lenny looked at Manny. "She get searched when she came in?"

"She's clean."

Honey of a Hurricane

Lenny looked back at Maile. "Come on, Tour Guide. Take me on a grand tour of the bedroom. That'll let you little friend off the hook."

Maile sat still, but kept her hand near the drink in case she needed to fling it in Lenny's eyes.

Lenny took a step closer to her. "What are you waiting for, Tour Guide?"

Maile knew the others were still watching her. She needed to make a decision. Either go in the bedroom with Lenny the snitch-turned-gangster, or suffer whatever his thugs might do to her. Or one of the others while they made her watch.

She looked over at Braces, who was still polishing the chrome plating on his pistol.

"Better do as the boss says, doll."

Maile looked at Manny. He had one hand in a pocket as if he was holding something bulky. With one last scan of the men around her, Higgs was slicing lemons for drinks with a long kitchen knife, the juice running out over the cutting board. Limps was leaning against a wall cleaning his fingernails with a pocketknife.

"Does she get the drink?"

"She can empty the bottle for all I care."

She put her hand on the drink and looked at Lenny. She made a decision. Pushing the drink back, Maile put one foot on the floor.

"Wait," Honey said from halfway across the living room. She stood from her easy chair, a little wobbly. She straightened her leather outfit. "I'll dance for you."

Lenny turned around. "How lucky for the tour guide. We have a volunteer."

Maile noticed Oscar whispering something to Santos, who nodded and pushed his wheelchair to the far side of the room.

"May I have the drink first?" Honey asked in a little girl's polite voice.

"Dance first, then the drink."

"But I don't have any music."

"Sing. You know how to sing, right? Or would you like the tour guide to sing for you?"

When Honey looked in her direction, Maile wasn't sure if her eyes were aimed at the drink on the bar or on her.

"I don't need music," Honey said.

As soon as Honey started her drunken gyrations, Maile silently prayed for it to end. Soon, her leather top was open, the chains swinging back and forth. The top dropped to the floor unceremoniously. Honey worked her hips, more clumsy than what an ex-cheerleader should be able to do. After a few minutes, Manny began to clap as though the performance was done. Braces and Higgs also clapped. Maile didn't realize she had closed her eyes during the performance.

Not bothering to clasp closed again, Honey went to the bar, her hand reaching for the drink before she got to it. Lenny beat her there and tossed the fluid away.

"Why?"

"That wasn't a performance. You'll get no pity drinks from me."

Honey sat on a barstool, almost missing it. "I'll do better if I have a drink first."

Lenny only looked at her, grinning as though he'd won a battle. That's when Honey took a swing at him, catching his face with a fingernail. He raised his hand to swing back, but Higgs put a bar towel in it. Lenny dabbed at the tiny scratch, once again acting as though he were seriously wounded, just like with the nick during his shave. He punctuated the drama with a soliloquy about women of the Hawaiian Islands.

Maile had seen enough. She went around to the back of the bar, uncorked a bottle, poured a drink, and set it on the bar. Honey lifted her head to look at it. A twitchy, nervous smile came to her face. "Thanks."

Honey took the glass, had a swallow, and retreated to the sofa with her prize in both hands. Maile left the bar and the gangsters behind, finding a sideboard to lean against in another part of the room. There was a display of beach shells that she mindlessly rearranged.

The wind was howling now, and the lights flickered.

"What happens if the lights go out?" Manny asked.

"Sit in the dark," Braces said, this time without laughing.

"Hey, Cripple, how bad can these storms get?" Lenny asked Oscar from across the room.

Oscar only waved derisively as he watched out the sliding glass doors.

Lenny went to Maile. "What about you, Tour Guide? Know anything about these kinds of storms?"

"Last hurricane we had in the islands hit the Big Island. Blew down power lines, uprooted trees, took roofs off houses."

"Old houses or new ones like this?"

"Storms don't care about how new or old the house is. It takes everything in its path, and doesn't stop until it's had its fill," Oscar said. "Dozen or so people were lost in that one, washed out to sea."

"What happened to them?"

"Some of their bodies were found on the beach a day or two later. Sharks got the rest."

"Where were they when the storm hit?" Lenny asked.

"Houses near the beach. Storm surge got them."

"Storm surge? What's that?"

"Like a tidal wave, only in slow motion. Nothing you can do about it but start swimming." Again, Oscar laughed without mirth. "Only problem with that is there's nowhere to swim to."

"You mean we could drown in here?" Lenny looked to be in as big of a panic as Maile had been all afternoon. "What about the neighbors? Why isn't someone doing something?"

"The smart one cleared out hours ago," Oscar said. "Only the dumb ones stay behind to ride it out." He pivoted his chair to look in Lenny's direction. "Dumb, like us."

Lenny went to windows on both sides of the house to look at the neighbors' places. "Why aren't there shutters on this place? A place like this should have shutters, I tell you."

"Shutters won't help, if the wind gets strong enough. Palm fronds and branches can fly for miles before they go through someone's window. Those things fly like artillery," Maile said. Since Lenny and a couple of the other gangsters were already unsettled, maybe she could push them into making a mistake. What that might be, she had no idea. All she knew was that things weren't going so well at the Swenberg house that night. "If they even have windows or a roof by then."

Lenny went back to Maile and stared her in the face. "Why are you here?"

"I wish I wasn't." Something hit a window and Maile looked in that direction. "Give me my phone and I'll leave."

"Why have I seen you at the police station?"

She looked back at him. "That's someone else."

"You're too classy to work the streets. You work the hotels?"

"Tour guide, I told you."

"Tour guides don't get taken in."

"You probably saw me on a tour."

Lenny paced a lap in the room before returning to her. "You know that Ota, don't you?"

"I don't know anybody's name."

"I think you're working for him. You're here on some sort of sting, right?"

"Not here on a police sting," she said. When she looked away, she noticed the others were closing in on them. "Just a working girl trying to earn a living."

"Who are you working for?"

"Not working for anyone."

"Who's your pimp?"

Maile didn't know any pimps personally, but knew the name of one. "Charles."

"The one with the Jaguar sedan?"

"Yeah."

"Small time hustler. I don't care about that guy."

"No one cares about you either, Lenny."

"Easy does it, doll," Manny warned quietly.

Lenny paced a lap around the room again, stalling in one corner. Maile didn't pay much attention to him, since Braces was looming close. "Shouldn't talk to the boss like that, Tour Guide. Not real healthy."

"One way to keep me quiet."

"What's that?" Braces asked.

"Give me my phone and let me leave."

"Fat chance, Tour Guide."

Lenny showed up. After looking Maile up and down, he stuck out his hand to Braces. "Where's your piece?"

Braces handed over his chrome pistol. Lenny already had a black pistol in his other hand. He stuck that in the palm of Maile's hand and stepped back from her.

"I heard a Hawaiian chick was being recruited to work for the feds. That's you, isn't it?"

Maile's halter-top felt tight on her chest as she tried to breathe. Lenny knew things, a lot of things. She'd been discovered, except she wasn't working for either the FBI or the Secret Service. She'd turned both agencies down, but as far as Lenny was concerned, that didn't matter. She had a gun in her hand, and another was aimed at her belly by a gangster.

"What do you want me to say?"

"That's as good as an admission of guilt," Lenny said. "Did Ota send you here or the feds?"

"Neither."

"Who sent you?"

Her heartbeat pounded in her ears. "No one. I told you, Suzie had me fill in for her today."

Lenny seemed to leer at her. "To kill me?"

Honey of a Hurricane

"Get over yourself. You're not worth going to prison for."

"You crashed this party for nothing?"

"I don't know why you're here and I don't care."

"Shoot him, Maile!" Oscar prompted.

"Yeah, shoot him!" Honey said.

Maile looked at the pistol in her hand and found it pointed at Lenny's breadbasket. Her finger was on the trigger. It felt as though it weighed a hundred pounds.

"Go ahead and shoot me, Tour Guide. The safety is off and the hammer is back." Lenny pulled back the hammer on the chrome-plated pistol he'd gotten from Braces. "All you have to do is pull the trigger."

Maile steadied her hand, and her grip on the gun. She didn't know how to shoot; she'd never handled a gun before.

"Shoot me, Tour Guide. That's what the others want."

Maile felt the trigger with the pad of her finger.

"That's right. All you have to do is press your finger on the trigger. Aim the gun at me and press the trigger."

Maile looked at his hand with the gun in it. His hand was steady and level, the gun aimed right at her.

"You'd be a hero to the police. I bet Detective Ota would even give you a reward for shooting me."

Maile lowered the gun and set it on the sideboard next to her. She walked away from it. When she saw Oscar, his head was hanging down again. With a glance at Honey, she was back to looking miserable while sipping her drink. She'd let them down by not killing the man that was brutally abusing them.

Honey of a Hurricane

Chapter Nine

Everyone in the house seemed to go to their own personal place for a respite. Two of the gangsters played cards on the bar while Braces polished his pistol. While Oscar sank deeper into a gloomy mood, Honey went for a swim in her glass of rum, and Santos settled her nerves by tidying the living room. Maile and Lenny, both now unarmed, went to opposite sides of the room to consider their stalemate.

Unwilling or unable to watch the storm outside, Maile took a seat on the couch next to Oscar. Even if the wheels were coming off the wagon inside the house, she still had her own personal agenda, and that was to find out what Oscar knew about the deaths of his brothers. Maybe he was guilty, maybe not, but Ota had put her in that room for a reason, and it wasn't to play games with Lenny.

Lenny paced a slow lap through the room, ending up back at the bar with his soldiers. "Get Mickey on the phone."

"Who, me?" Braces asked.

"No, Tinkerbell, you idiot." Lenny looked at Manny. "Find Mickey. We should've heard from them by now."

Oscar shook his head over what he and Maile had heard. "Should've been out of the house by now."

"Shoulda shot 'em when you had the chance," Honey said, with drunken speech.

"Nobody's getting shot, not tonight," Maile said.

"Didn't want to be a hero, or didn't have the guts to be one?" Oscar asked.

"Hero's got nothing to do with it. Nobody needs to die."

"Better a live coward than a dead hero," Honey muttered. She looked up from her glass. "Sorry. Didn't mean for it to sound that way."

With an empty glass in her hand, Honey left her perch and went off in search of a refill.

Maile couldn't put it off any longer. She needed something out of Oscar, one way or another. She'd been sent to get some dirt on Frank Swenberg's murder, and if Oscar had anything to do with it. The way things looked right then, Oscar might not survive the night, if Lenny and his gang hung around much longer.

"Look, I don't know what's going on here at the house tonight," Maile told him. She leaned close to talk privately, while Lenny concerned himself with his call to someone named Mickey. "Detective Ota sent me here to talk to you."

"No he didn't."

Maile looked across the room to where Lenny was still on the phone, now arguing about something. His gang was more concerned with the phone call than with Honey emptying the bottle of rum into her tumbler. "All I know is that Ota has his own agenda."

"What's that?" Oscar asked.

"He still thinks you have something to do with Frank's death."

Oscar looked at Lenny for a moment. "In a way, I do. But I can't tell him that unless I want to go to prison."

"He thinks you killed him, either directly or indirectly."

"Maybe he's right." Oscar changed position in his chair. Braces had been walking a slow lap around the room, stalling nearby to polish his gun. Oscar continued as if he didn't care who was listening. "I hadn't seen either of them in years, maybe decades. Then all of a sudden, Carl shows up on my front porch, asking for help."

"Business help or help with trouble?" Maile asked.

"Both. But I was able to get rid of him, at least for a while. Then Frank showed up, again with the same request that I bail both of them out of trouble."

"Why didn't you help them? Granted, they were only half-brothers, but still flesh and blood, right?"

"They were the California side of the family, and had always excluded me from everything for as long as I could remember. It was like those people who win the lottery and all of a sudden, relatives come out of the woodwork looking for a handout. I wasn't giving it to them."

Braces continued his lap around the room and got back to the bar.

"How much did they want?"

"They needed a million, each."

"Do you have it?" she asked.

"I'd have to move a few things around, maybe sell off some stock I no longer care about, but I could've come up with it, yeah."

"What kind of trouble were they in?" Just then, Lenny slammed the phone down onto the bar, cursing. Braces had a quick chat with Lenny, who looked at Maile, and nodded. That's when it dawned on Maile, what was going on that night. "Don't tell me. Lenny had something to do with your brothers' trouble?"

"A lot to do with it."

Lenny swaggered from the bar to the middle of the large room where Maile and Oscar were talking. His lackeys trailed behind, with Honey bringing up the rear. Her gait had lost that model's walk, and she was simply trying to get one foot ahead of the other without spilling her drink. When the troupe got there, Manny was sent out to check the backyard.

"Go ahead, Oscar," Lenny said. "Tell the tour guide what your brothers' trouble was. Tell her who was behind their trouble."

Oscar tossed his head in Lenny's direction. "He had everything to do with it."

Maile didn't dare look up at Lenny's face. "What happened?"

"You want me to tell her, Oscar?" Lenny said with a laugh. "You look a little dispirited."

Oscar simply waved his hand as though he didn't care.

Manny came in then, drenched with rain. The captain of their chartered boat had come with him. "Look who I found untying his lines."

"What's going on, Cap'n?"

"Please, sir. The weather is too bad for the boat to be tied up to such a small dock. I should take it out to deeper water."

"You're not going anywhere. I hired you for a week, and I still have two more days."

"Please, sir, it's the weather. There's too much wind. The hull, it is getting damaged."

"I don't care if your boat is sinking."

"Please, sir…"

His gaze locked onto the captain's eyes, Lenny held out his hand to Braces. "Gimme."

Braces slapped his pistol into Lenny's hand, who then aimed it in the captain's face. He took the captain's wet raincoat in his fist and pulled him close. "Move that boat one inch and you're a dead man, got it?"

The captain pretended to salute. "Yes, sir."

"Get outta here. Get the boat ready. We'll be leaving pretty soon." Lenny pushed him back, propelling him to the back door. Lenny looked at Manny again. "Change your clothes and bring the stuff. Mickey should be here soon."

"Finally, you're leavin'," Honey said. Her pronunciation barely made sense.

"We're leaving when were good and ready to." Lenny looked back at Oscar. "Go ahead and tell the tour guide what happened to your brothers."

Oscar sat staring at the floor in front of him.

"I'll tell her. The tour guide has one last tour to go on. She has a right to know."

"What do you mean, one last tour?" Maile asked.

"Don't ask that," Honey said. "You don't want to know."

"You're coming with us, Tour Guide. And it'll be a one-way trip, so don't bother packing."

Maile knew what that meant and didn't want to think about it. Now she had a new objective, to form an escape plan. Getting the story of Carl and Frank Swenberg's deaths was now secondary to getting out of the house alive, and not going on a one-way boat trip during a hurricane with gangsters.

Only one thought crossed her mind: if it was better to take a bullet on dry land or out to sea.

"You see, it's like this," Lenny said. "Oscar here found himself a new prospect named Laurie Long. He found her, in all places, working the corner of Hotel Street and Maunakea, across the street from Wo Fat's. Guess what she was doing?"

Honey left them and wandered off in the direction of the bar. Going to the back, she poured a tall glass of whisky and sat there, glass in one hand, bottle in the other.

"When Oscar found out she had a tidy little nest egg saved up, he dreamt up a plan of how to get it out of her. He must've sold her the flashiest sales package he had, because two weeks later, she was cleaned up. And I mean she was shiny clean. She'd been to the doctor for a shot of penicillin, had a trip to the dentist, a visit at the salon, and a daylong shopping trip in Waikiki with her new personal fashion manager. Of course, they were of Oscar's choosing, and he got kickbacks from all of them. She was even off the booze."

"What's she got to do with the Swenberg brothers?" Maile asked.

"Everything. Once Laurie had transformed, she needed a new name. That was what she thought about on her flight to LA to meet her new talent agent. By the time she landed at LAX, she was no longer Laurie Long, Honolulu hooker, but Honey Thrust, LA's newest actress and wannabe porn star."

Honey of a Hurricane

Maile looked over at Honey, who had her head down on the bar. Maybe she was asleep, maybe she was crying quietly, Maile couldn't be sure.

"Well, that agent schlepped Honey from one end of LA to the other, trying to get anything on film for her. They all liked the look of her but she couldn't act, couldn't learn her lines, didn't read well in auditions, couldn't even find her mark."

It was another character assassination being performed by Lenny at the expense of someone's self-respect. Not that there was a whole lot of respect in that house that night.

"Then she got her big break. Her last chance came in a house that was set up as a studio out in the San Fernando Valley. They asked her to audition for a lead part in a short film that might turn into a serial. Her first clue should've come when she didn't have a script to read from. When her leading man arrived on the set naked, she finally started to piece things together. But bless her heart, she went with it.

"She performed well enough that they offered her the female lead in the first three films in their porno serial. They even liked her stage name of Honey Thrust. All she had to do was sign on the dotted line."

"Yee hee! Porn star!" laughed Braces.

Lenny pointed his thumb at Braces. "Finally he finds something funny to laugh about."

"I still don't see what that has to do with the Swenbergs?" Maile asked. "Where were you, Oscar?"

"Oh, he stayed behind in Hawaii. All he ever did was watch the budget, which was mostly Honey's money earned on her back in Chinatown."

"So, she made some pornos. Big deal. How did Carl and Frank get involved?" Maile asked.

"She made ten pornos altogether. But that wasn't the problem, was it, Oscar?"

"Take your money and get lost," Oscar mumbled.

Maile was starting to piece things together. Oscar's house was up for sale because of Honey.

"Soon enough. You see, Honey was supposed to buy into the series of films, for a cut in the profits. She didn't have the money, and when she asked Oscar for it, he sent her to Carl, right there in LA. He went back to Oscar, who still didn't want to buy into his client's career, but he sent Carl and Honey to me for a loan. It sounded like a good deal, so I handed over the money, for fifty percent of her take, along with repayment in two years. That was three years ago and I still haven't seen a dime."

"You're not the first loan shark to not get paid back," Oscar said.

"But he's the first one to let someone live so long. Remember that, Cripple," Manny said.

Lenny took over. "Then just as she was making some decent money acting in her pornos, the production company made a new offer, that for more money, they could make ten more films for a total of twenty. Same deal, but she still didn't have enough money. That's when she showed up on my doorstep again, this time with Frank, their hands out. Call me a sucker, but I had them sign another agreement."

"How much was it?" Maile asked.

"A million per contract. In only three months' time, she'd burned through her savings and was two million deep in debt."

"To a loan shark," Oscar said.

"She's still alive, ain't she?"

"My brothers aren't."

"As if you care about them."

"Didn't have to murder them," Oscar said, angling his wheelchair away.

"The only reason Honey's alive is that I can still recover some of my losses with her. You're not worth two million, remember that, Oscar."

"I have the house for sale."

"For sale isn't money in my pocket," Lenny said.

Maile had most of her answer for Ota, that Lenny was somehow responsible for the death of either or both Swenberg brothers. Maybe he didn't plunge the knife or inject poison, but he would've directed someone to do his dirty work for him. Most likely, that person was in the room with them. Other than pushing Honey into an even deeper hole than she'd already dug for herself, Oscar was mostly innocent of crime. But there was two million dollars that needed to be repaid, and maybe that's what this Mickey person was all about.

Maile wasn't sure if she wanted Mickey to show up or not. If he was turning over two million to repay Honey's debt to Lenny, that got a lot of people out of hot water. But it also meant it would be time for Lenny and his thugs to leave Honolulu, apparently on the fishing boat, and with Maile going with them for a one-way tour of hurricane tidal swells.

Maile had to find a way out. Ota wasn't expecting her at the transit center until she called, and she was overdue. She was supposed to be in the house for only four hours, and that was long past. She wondered where he was, if he'd given up on her and went back to town, or was still waiting. Lenny, or one of his lackeys, still had all their phones, so there was no way to call for help. She needed to find a way out, and most of all, not get on that boat.

The lights flickered again before going out altogether.

"What's wrong?" Lenny asked, looking around the room in the dark.

"Storm knocked out the lights," Oscar said.

"So, what? We just stand here in the dark?" Braces asked.

Santos showed up with candles and a battery lamp. Once the candles were lit, she took one back to the bar. This time, Maile followed her.

"Pour a drink, Maile," Honey said.

"Thanks, but I'm okay."

"Teetotaler?"

"Tonight I am. Which might turn out to be a bad decision."

"There're sodas in the fridge."

Maile looked and found another ginger ale. There were also Rocky Road candy bars. She got one of each, and poured her ginger ale in a glass. She used a kitchen knife to cut the candy bar into six pieces.

"Metal handle kitchen knife," she muttered.

"Yeah, so?" Honey slurred.

Honey of a Hurricane

Maile went through the drawers at the bar, not finding any others similar to the metal handled one she was holding. "Are there more of these? A set?"

"In the kitchen. One's missin'."

"A long paring knife?"

"Filet knife," Honey said, resting her head on the bar again. "How'd you know?"

"Just a guess."

Higgs came to the bar and wrenched the knife from Maile's hand, taking it with him to another room.

Taking the soda and the candy bar, Maile sat on a bar stool next to Honey, their only light the flickering candle between them.

"Is what Lenny said true?" Maile asked.

"Mostly." Honey took a sip of her drink. "For once, he's not lying about something."

"You owe him two million dollars?"

Honey held up three fingers.

"Three million?"

Honey nodded while taking a sip of her drink.

"You have anything in the bank?"

Honey shook her head. "That's why I'm shacked up with Oscar."

"You could go home."

"To my parents' house? Forget it. They want nothing to do with me. I got myself a rep when I started turning tricks in Chinatown."

"You had a rep a long time before then. But never mind that. What does Lenny want you to do to pay off your loans?"

"He's selling me to this Mickey guy that's on his way."

"Selling?" Maile asked.

"Mickey is taking over my contract. He has connections in LA. Supposedly." Honey took a drink. "I'm going back to LA to make more pornos to pay off my contract."

"How long will it take to pay it off?" Maile asked. "Three million sounds like a lot of money."

"At least a couple of years, and I get nothing out of it. I got myself a rep in LA, also."

"From making those films?" Maile asked.

Honey held up her glass. "From too much of this and too many bail bonds that still need to be paid back to my old agent."

"Your parents wouldn't happen to have three million dollars to help you out?"

"Not likely."

"And you're shacked up with Oscar because you might be able to get it from him?"

"Didn't take long for you to figure that out, but he doesn't have it either. Unless he sells this stupid house and his boat in the next hour."

"Why is all this taking place at the house tonight?"

"They think Oscar and I are together."

"Aren't you? I thought you were engaged?" Maile asked. "That's what you told me a while back."

"That party was meant to get me discovered again. There were agents and producers there that day, legit ones, not all that smut stuff. We thought if we pretended to be engaged, it would elevate my stock as an actress, that the industry players would take me seriously."

"Didn't happen?"

"Not even a nibble."

"Sorry."

"Not your fault. It's my fault Oscar sold my contract to Lenny in the first place."

"You're not merchandise, Laurie. They can't just sell you back and forth like that."

Hearing her real name seemed to catch the girl by surprise. "Don't call me that. Laurie Long's soul died a long time ago, and Honey Thrust uses her body now."

"I think there's still some Laurie deep down inside of you, wanting to come out again."

"Fat chance on ever seeing her again." Honey ate the last piece of the marshmallow candy. "Shouldn't be eating this. I need to lose eight pounds by the time I'm back in LA."

"For the films?"

Honey nodded. "Filming starts next month. Each film takes three days to tape, then I get a day off before making the next one. Go to the suntan booth, get a facial, take a laxative, whatever. Six weeks of that, then a week off to rest before starting a new series. It'll take a year of that, maybe two, before they're done with me."

"That's a lot of…I'm not sure of how to put it," Maile said. While they talked, she picked through spray-glued snags in her hair.

"Porn."

"I don't see how you can keep…interested?"

"They give me stuff. Not drink, but other stuff."

"What other stuff?" Maile asked. She had a good idea of what.

"We do one rehearsal with our clothes on, then they give me a roofie to keep me interested, to make my body react for the camera. It's not so bad, because I never remember much of what happened."

"Those drugs are addictive, Laurie."

"No kidding. That's why I drink so much of this." Honey nudged Maile's elbow. "That's why I told you to drink out of cans while you're here, and not to take a drink from that Higgs guy."

"They're giving you roofies here, also?"

"When I perform for Lenny. Not today, though. I have to travel later, and be able to walk to do it."

Maile was forming a plan of escape. "Who keeps them? Higgs?"

"At first. He got me a little too stoned the first night they were here. That was the night they busted up Oscar. They said I went with him and Manny to the hospital, made some sort of scene there, but I don't remember nothin' of it."

"Who has them?"

"The nurse. They think it's safer if a nurse gives them to me, then watches over me later until I wake up. Same with Suzie and the other girls that have been here." Honey took a sip of whisky. "Sometimes, I wish…"

"Wish what?" Maile asked quietly.

"Nothing."

"I've never seen any, but don't those films get repetitive?" Maile asked, changing the subject.

"They keep the films interesting by using different men, changing my hair and makeup, different sets and outfits, fake tattoos. A couple of the series might involve other women. But at least I won't be in debt to that Mickey guy when I'm done."

"If you last that long. Laurie, you need to find a way out of that."

"It's either make the films or suffer."

"He'd kill you?" Maile asked in a whisper.

"Or worse."

"What's worse than dead?"

"Go ask Oscar that. He's the cripple in that wheelchair over there."

A fist pounded on the front door, interrupting the palms beating against the walls outside.

"Probably Mickey and the boys," Lenny said. "Go let them in."

Manny opened the door, letting wind blow through the house. Candles flickered wildly and a few went out. It wasn't the man Lenny was waiting for, but a neighbor that Maile recognized from an earlier visit to the house. He was dripping wet and carrying a large flashlight. Oblivious to what was going on, he nodded to Lenny and his henchmen on his way to Oscar in his wheelchair.

"Sorry to interrupt your party, Oscar, but the lights have gone out."

"Yee hee! The lights are out!" Braces said, laughing.

"We hadn't noticed," Lenny said, walking away.

The neighbor shrugged it off. "I put in a call to the electric company, and they said it'll be a few hours before they're on again."

"Thanks. Maybe you should go tell the other neighbors," Oscar told him.

"On my way. I see your friends' boat left the channel for open water. Smart move."

Lenny snapped his fingers at Manny to go outside to the dock to check.

"Want me to check on your yacht?" the neighbor offered.

"I have it tied up solid. It should be okay."

"We might be taking it out in a while," Lenny said.

"Wait till the storm passes. A yacht like that isn't built for seas like we're getting tonight. I doubt you'd make it through the channel to open water in these winds."

Lenny swaggered over to him. "You're the neighborhood Boy Scout?"

"Neighborhood watch captain."

"Look, Boy Scout. We'll take care of our business, and you take care of everyone else's. Now, why don't you run along like a good little Boy Scout and check on the rest of the campground?"

"Yeah, sure, alright." He looked past Lenny toward Oscar. "I heard about a couple of bank robbers that might've come this way. Filipino guys. I wonder if they took your friend's fishing boat?"

"Yeah, sure, fella," Lenny said, aiming the neighbor for the door. "Why don't you be a good Boy Scout and go look for them?"

With a shrug, the neighbor flicked on his flashlight when he got to the door and went back out into the storm. Manny shut the door behind him.

Nurse Santos got the candles lit again, just as there was another knock on the front door.

"Now who?" Lenny asked, watching Manny open the door again. "Girl Scouts selling cookies?"

Maile and Honey both watched to see who it was.

Honey of a Hurricane

Honey swore under her breath when a woman walked into the room. Four men came with her. She handed off her dripping umbrella.

"Uh oh," Maile whispered, when she saw who it was.

Chapter Ten

Lenny walked across the room, looking genuinely happy for the first time all night. "Mickey!"

"Lenny Gallo! It's been forever and a day. When was the last time we did business?"

"A few years ago. That jockey at Hollywood Park, remember?"

Mickey scanned the faces in the room for a second time. "That little twerp. He brought five horses in and never won another race, even when they were fixed. A year later, he wasn't even making his weight. Sorry I ever bought him."

"Where is he now?" Lenny asked. They were at the bar, where Lenny poured both of them shots under the watchful eye of Honey. Instead of trying to hide, Maile decided to watch Mickey closely. She was certain she'd been noticed by the woman.

"Poor fellow had himself a barn mishap when he got kicked to death by the last horse he ever rode. That's what the police thought, anyway." Mickey looked closely at Lenny as she slugged her shot. "What happened to your face?"

He used a cocktail napkin to blot both the shaving nick and the scratch Honey left behind. "Women."

Mickey laughed. "Same old Lenny. Got the contract?"

"Got the money?"

Mickey snapped her fingers. One of her men brought a gym bag that was set on the bar and zipped it open. While that went on, Limps cleaned his fingernails while one of Mickey's men watched him. To Maile's eye, their posturing was simple, but deadly.

Lenny went through the same procedure with Honey's acting contract.

"Is she here?" Mickey asked.

"At the end of the bar..." Lenny looked at the empty bottle on the bar. "...and at the end of her bottle."

Mickey looked at Honey. "Mind standing? I need to see the goods."

Honey slipped off her stool and stood before the woman.

"Sugar, if it's not too much trouble, strip." When Honey delayed, Mickey cleared her throat. "From what I've heard, you know how."

Honey let her leather outfit fall to the floor and turned a circle, staggering through the simple move.

"Lay off the booze and chocolate bars," Mickey said, going back to reading the contract.

Maile helped Honey get dressed again, a monumental chore for as simple as the outfit was.

"You alright?" Maile asked.

"Better than you."

"Why?"

"I'm gonna live long enough to see the sun come up."

While Mickey had her man read the contract, Lenny and his boys counted bills. It took all of ten minutes to accomplish both.

But those ten minutes felt like an eternity to Maile. The entire time, she and Mickey stared at each other. Mickey might've been a broker of flesh from LA, but she was also known as Special Agent Michelle Hartzel of the FBI, supposedly conducting an investigation into human trafficking. Maile wondered if this was the operation Hartzel had asked her to be a part of.

But Hartzel was the one doing the trafficking, and Lenny was making out like a pig wallowing in a sty full of fresh slop. That was the part that didn't make sense. If she was a straight federal agent, she wouldn't have brought Maile into an operation as risky as this. If she was dirty, Maile should have a bullet in her forehead by now. Maile couldn't figure it out, but right then, Hartzel, or Mickey, wasn't any more trustworthy than anyone else in the house that night.

"What're the two of you looking at?" Lenny asked, when he noticed the staring match.

"Nothing," Maile said, now looking away.

"Who's this one? Someone new?" Mickey asked.

"No one you want," Lenny said.

"Why not? I could put her to work."

"You don't want her, I said. She's coming with me."

"Give you a hundred grand for her."

"Two hundred, and I want legit cash," Lenny said.

"Two-fifty of what you just gave me. You know it's good stuff."

"Three hundred."

"I'm not for sale," Maile said, leaving her bar stool. She needed to do something. She was hoping Hartzel was trying to get her out of a bad deal of going with Lenny, maybe suspecting what was coming her way later. She also felt a little insulted, that Honey had been bought for three million dollars, and Maile was worth only a couple hundred thousand.

One of Mickey's men stepped in front of Maile. He was easily twice her size, built like a linebacker.

"For three hundred, I want to check the merchandise first," Mickey said.

"Suit yourself," Lenny said, going back to inspecting the cash from Mickey.

"Take the dress off," Mickey told Maile.

Maile frowned. "No. You can see enough the way I am."

"Take it off or it'll be taken off of you." When Maile continued to hesitate, Mickey nodded at the linebacker bodyguard. "Do it."

When she felt large hands on her shoulders, Maile reached back to tug down the zipper of her halter-top. She held it in her hand after it was off and continued to face Mickey. At least it was a woman sizing her up and not Lenny.

"And the skirt."

That left Maile in a bra and undies with pantyhose, and still wondering if it was all a charade being put on by Mickey to get her out of the house and away from Lenny. With all the running she'd been doing lately, Maile knew she was in top shape.

"What's your name?" Mickey asked.

Maile wasn't sure of how to answer.

"We call her Tour Guide," Lenny muttered. "You don't want her. Doesn't know how to keep her big trap shut."

"How old are you, Tour Guide?"

"Twenty-seven."

Mickey went back to the bar and poured another shot for herself. "Never mind. Too old. I could get two or three years out of her, tops. Not even worth a hundred grand." She slugged back her shot. "Next time, find me something younger, Lenny."

Santos came over to help Maile, who couldn't dress fast enough. Not only was she insulted by being labeled as too old to act in porn, she wasn't being rescued from the house.

"Everything look okay, Manny?" Lenny asked his partner.

"First rate stuff, boss." Manny was using a single eye jeweler's loupe to inspect the money close-up. Apparently, it was counterfeit cash, and everyone was aware of it. "Paper feels okay, right ink, good lines, serial numbers are good."

Santos went to where Manny was inspecting bills and picked one up. "Never seen so many hundreds in one place."

Braces yanked the bill from her hand and set it back in the pile again. "No tips for nurses."

Santos shrugged and took a single step back, still watching as money was inspected.

Once Manny was done, he gave a nod, proclaiming it to be top quality. Lenny looked at Mickey. "We're done?"

Mickey smiled at him. "Nice doing business with you, Lenny."

While Lenny and his thugs went about the task of recounting the cash, Maile watched as Honey went toward the bedroom.

"Where are you going?" Maile asked Honey as she joined Mickey and her men. She had a suitcase in one hand. With the way Maile hadn't been rescued by

Mickey—Agent Hartzel—the woman had to be a dirty federal agent. Honey really was going back to LA, just like Maile was headed to sea with Lenny and his gang. "You're going with them?"

"No, duh. I've been paid for. I go where I'm told."

"You don't have to go with them. You can't be bought like that."

"See what I mean?" Lenny said. "Too dumb to keep quiet. That's why she's coming with us."

"Don't go, Laurie. We can find money to buy your way out of your trouble."

"Stay out of it, Tour Guide."

"Yeah, that's nice, but this storm isn't going away any time soon," Mickey said.

Maile watched as Honey got in line, with two men in front, two behind, and Mickey bringing up the rear, popping up her umbrella as she left the house. Limps was there to close the door after they were gone.

Maile looked over at Oscar, who still had his head down. Santos was standing behind the bar in silence.

"Now, we need to figure out what to do with you, Tour Guide."

Chapter Eleven

As much as nobody liked storms, Maile had a deep appreciation for the one that was still raging outside. As long as that wind blew, the ocean would stay too choppy to get the yacht out of the channel to open water. That gave her more time to figure a way out of her predicament.

The evening was grinding on her nerves, though. She found herself holding her breath anytime Lenny spoke, and her heartbeat raced whenever one of the men came near. Nurse Santos was like Switzerland, not taking up sides, and mostly being ignored. Maile felt alone, deserted, with one less woman in the house. She did her best to keep Lenny's promise out of her mind.

One way or another, Lenny wasn't ready to leave the house yet. Either he was afraid of going out in the weather, or he had some other task to complete. That would have something to do with her or Oscar Swenberg, who had sunk into despair. Santos was still there, but as Swenberg's nurse, she shouldn't have concerned Lenny too much. Her fate, and that of Swenberg, hadn't been discussed.

Unless there was going to be a mass murder of all three witnesses to Honey being sold to Mickey. But Maile couldn't figure the point of that; it simply wasn't that big of a crime that needed to be hidden. If buying and selling her contract was even a crime. It was only business, after all, and Honey was simply the collateral that supported it. No, there was more to that night than just an odd business deal made during a storm.

Honey of a Hurricane

Maile crossed her arms and put her attention on Lenny. "Okay, you did your business deal with your friend. Why aren't you leaving?"

"What's the hurry, Tour Guide?"

"I don't understand why you're not leaving. You've got your money, the contract has been paid. Time for you to leave Oscar alone."

"Sit down, girlie," Manny said behind Maile. A hand pushed her down into a chair.

While wind blew and rain pattered against windows, Lenny started pacing again. "Not so easy as that."

"I guess I don't understand why not."

Lenny leaned over to look in her face. "No, you don't. That's because you just walked in. You should've found a john and stayed out of this mess. Or better yet, stayed home with your mother, instead of leaving her all alone in her little house."

Maile got a shiver. Lenny knew where her mother lived. She had left her brother Kenny to stay with her mother during the storm, but that didn't mean other harm couldn't find them. Lenny was right. She should've stayed home that day. More than ever, she wanted her phone to call them.

"She's just fine. Both she and the house have been through bigger storms than this. Right now, you seem more obsessed with me than anything else."

"Yeah, you know why?"

"Because you're unbalanced?"

"Careful, girlie," Manny muttered behind her.

"Everything will come into balance once I have one last piece of the puzzle. And you have the key to that."

Another shiver. She knew exactly what he meant. "I do?"

"Where are the keys, Tour Guide?"

"What keys?"

Lenny walked a slow lap through the living room, looking out windows at the storm as he went.

"This place needs shutters, I tell you. Who builds a house and doesn't put shutters on the windows."

"It's okay, boss. This place is solid," Manny said. He didn't sound convinced.

With the way the house shuddered in the wind, Maile wasn't so sure either. She had more faith in her mother's little cottage than she did in Swenberg's home.

Lenny stopped in front of Maile. "Where are the keys?"

"What keys do you mean?"

"Keys to the safe deposit boxes."

That was an answer to a question that been haunting Maile, and Detective Ota, for weeks. She had met Frank Swenberg at the beach during a tour, and later saved him from drowning in the waves. He had taken something into the ocean with him that day, a simple box. When he was pulled out by lifeguards, he no longer had the box. Eventually, through a series of odd occurrences, Maile recovered the box from Oscar's yacht. She never had learned how the box got from a head of coral at the beach to the Swenberg yacht, but she was finally discovering what might be inside the box, or at least how valuable it might be.

"You can look at the keys on my key ring. I have a lot of keys. Maybe your safe deposit box keys are on it?"

Lenny looked at Manny for an answer.

"Already checked, boss. Not on there. Nowhere in her bag."

Lenny leaned down to look her in the eyes again. "Where are my keys, Tour Guide?"

When she smelled his breath, she caught the scent of the shots he'd had with Mickey earlier. That mixed with the menthol shave cream that Santos had used to shave his face, and Honey's lingering patchouli. "I don't have them, my mother doesn't have them, and evidently Oscar doesn't have them. Otherwise, you would've found them here in the house and you'd be gone by now."

"Yee hee! What a mess!" Braces laughed. "We turned this place upside-down when we got here, and that yacht. Nothing."

Lenny finally sat on the couch opposite from Maile. He still wasn't relaxed, though, as he sat fidgeting. The storm was beginning to take its toll on his nerves.

"The keys were supposed to have been transferred from the Swenberg brothers to Oscar. Then he was supposed to hand them over to me. Instead of making it a simple drop, ol' Frank made a theatrical performance of the deal. He put the keys in a box and attempted making the transfer underwater at Hanauma Beach."

"Bay," Maile said to correct him. It was simply a stall so she could try to remember exactly what went on that day at the beach. "Hanauma Bay."

"Whatever, Tour Guide. But that box went into the water and never came out again, that we could see. You know that, and we know you know that, because you were seen there that day. Frank bought sodas from you on the beach, and then you pulled that fancy maneuver later in the water."

"What maneuver? He never gave me any box."

"Blowing in his mouth. Very dramatic."

"Mouth-to-mouth resuscitation? Nothing fancy about that. Dramatic, but not fancy."

"Stick to the subject of the box. I think you know where it is."

"If you were there watching that day, you'd know I got out of the water right after the lifeguards pulled Frank out, and had nothing in my hands."

"Maybe you went back for it later?"

These were the same questions Detective Ota had asked her, numerous times already. She knew where the box was, but she wasn't leading him to it, any more than she was turning it over to Ota. As it was, the box was only steps from where her mother lived, and she wasn't taking Lenny anywhere near there, that night or any other night. Lenny already had three hostages; she wasn't going to turn her mother and brother into victims also.

"The box probably got lost in the sand, or the current dragged it out to sea." Maile shrugged. "It could be anywhere by now. Who knows? Maybe this storm will toss it up onto the beach? Maybe you should go look for it there."

"Knock off the wise guy stuff, girlie," Manny said.

Lenny was slowly turning into a neurotic mess, with his face beginning to twitch with each blow of the storm. "That would almost be a good answer, but I know better."

"Yeah, girlie," Manny said. "When we tossed the place, we found the discs that record all the video from the security cameras here. Oscar's very good at labeling and keeping them, one disc per day. They go back years. Well, we looked at them, and guess what?"

Maile knew what was coming. "I have no idea of what you're talking about."

"I think you do. We found a few images of Oscar bringing that box home, and then taking it to his yacht. When he came out again, he no longer had the box."

"So, there's your answer. Go search the yacht."

"We did. You know what we found?"

"Evidently not the box."

"Very good, Tour Guide," Lenny said, taking the conversation back again. "We also watched more security images. This is the part that'll interest you. We found images of someone dressed in black sneak into the yacht the very next night. It was a woman, just about your size and shape, Tour Guide. Isn't that right, fellas?"

"Yee hee!" Braces laughed. As he had been all evening, he was polishing his chrome-plated pistol. "Built just like you."

"How many women on this island are built like me?" Maile asked.

"Some. But the one in the security pictures had the same length hair, and did some very athletic stuff. A woman would have to be in very good condition to do some of the things that prowler did that night."

"That's why we had you strip earlier. Nothing personal. We just needed to see your physique," Manny said. "You're not just slender, you're athletic, just the kind of body someone would need to prowl around the yard and the yacht, leaping from one place to another."

"You took the box with you that night, Tour Guide. Where is it?"

The corner Maile was being backed into was feeling crowded. "Gave it to the police. What else would I do with it?"

Lenny looked as though he were having a stroke. "Were the keys inside?"

"I don't know. It was locked."

"You didn't try picking it?"

"I'm a tour guide. What do I know about picking locks?"

"You can jump over fences and crawl along the top of walls, leap from the dock to the boat and back again, search the boat, and steal something, but you can't figure out how to pick a simple lock? What are you, stupid?"

That was something she didn't like being called. "Sorry I'm so dumb. Maybe the key that opens the box was with the keys that were locked in the box?"

"What? That makes no sense."

"Neither does anything else tonight."

At some point, Nurse Santos had gone to the bar and was putting stoppers in bottles. Maybe she knew something Maile didn't, but several shots had been poured, waiting on the bar to be drunk.

"You really expect me to believe you turned the box over to Ota?"

"Yes."

"You think I don't have friends in the police department?"

"Believe it or not, I really do have better things to think about than you."

"Careful, girlie," Manny said.

"I had the evidence locker checked, and nothing even remotely similar to a box was signed into evidence by Ota or anyone else. And knowing what a conscientious fool Ota is, I know he would've signed something in. That means you still have it."

"Maybe I threw it away?"

"Why go to all the trouble of stealing the thing if you were only going to throw it away later?"

"So Oscar couldn't have it." Of all the lies she'd been telling in the last few hours, that one was the least deceptive.

Lenny paced another lap, again looking out windows at the weather. From what Maile could hear, the storm was beginning to pass, not a good thing for her right then. Lenny made his way back to Maile.

"For the last time, where's the box?" he asked.

"And for the last time, I don't know."

"Tell me now. If you do, we'll go get it. If we find it, we'll let you go."

"Might not be in good shape," Manny said. "But you'd be alive."

"Yee hee!" Braces said. "Tour guide goin' on a tour of the hospital!"

Lenny waited until the others were done with their threats. "If you don't tell me, you're going on the yacht with us. Take your pick."

If she told him the box was hidden in the Manoa House next door to her mother's cottage, she'd lead him right to her. If she kept lying about not knowing where it was, it would put her on the boat. If they killed her, they might still go to her mother's cottage and search there. There were no good alternatives.

She'd need to take her chances of making a run for it on the way to the yacht. It was still dark, and if she managed to dive into the channel without getting shot, and if she dealt with the choppy water, she might just survive. That was all she could think of for an escape plan.

"I'm sorry. I wish I could give you the keys to your safe deposit box, but I don't have them."

"Braces, Higgs, get our things. We're leaving."

"Boss, the weather," Manny said.

"Not so bad now. It'll be light in a couple of hours. We need to get a few miles between us and the Coast Guard before they launch a search."

"They have a helicopter and planes. We'll need more than just a couple of hour's head start."

Lenny went to Oscar and gave his face a slap. "Hey, Cripple. You and the nurse won't call the cops after we leave, right?"

"I don't care about you."

Lenny held his hand out to Manny. "Gimme."

Manny put his pistol in Lenny's hand, who then pressed it against Oscar's forehead.

"Go ahead," Oscar said. "I've got nothing to lose."

Lenny laughed. "That's right, you don't. You were selling this house and the yacht to get the money to buy Honey's contract from me. Now Mickey's got the contract and the girl, and you're in a wheelchair. In one bad deal, you really sold yourself out, Cripple. But I still don't want you or the nurse to call the cops, got it?"

"We won't."

"What happens if you do?" Manny asked. "We've talked about that. Remember what we agreed on?"

"Someone comes back to burn the house, and I go back to the hospital," Oscar mumbled.

"And why would you be going back to the hospital?"

"I'd be in the house when it burned."

Lenny slowly eased the muzzle off Oscar's forehead and gave the gun back to Manny. "Just to be sure, we're taking the phones with us, and leaving the two of you tied up and gagged."

After Lenny nodded at his thugs to tie up Santos and Oscar, he went to the bar.

"What's all this?" he asked, looking at the shot glasses.

"The ocean will still be choppy," Santos said. "I put out seasick pills for each of you and a shot of whisky to wash it down."

"Very thoughtful of you, Nurse." Lenny picked up a small white pill and gave it a careful look. "Now here's someone who knows how to cooperate. Want to come with us?"

"I need to stay with Mister Swenberg."

"Have it your way, Nurse. I could use someone with smarts like yours in the group."

Maile was surprised when Lenny tossed back the pill and washed it down with his shot of whisky. She suspected there was more to those pills and shots of whisky than met the eye. Once Oscar and the nurse were bound and gagged, Lenny had each of his thugs take a pill.

"There's one here for you, Tour Guide."

"I don't get seasick."

"You're taking it anyway. If it's good enough for us, it's good enough for you."

Maile went to the bar. Looking at the pill, it was too big to be the usual motion sickness medicine that would be bought over the counter. She also recognized the manufacturer's logo on it, and knew it was prescription. Wondering if Santos had somehow slipped all of them a mickey by handing out roofies instead of seasick pills, she cheeked the pill and swallowed the shot. Somehow, she'd have to find a way of spitting it out without being seen, and before it dissolved.

"Tie her hands," Lenny said. "I don't trust that one."

Braces began to tie Maile's hands with the same cord they used on Oscar and Santos.

"No. Use something else. When the Coast Guard fishes her body out of the drink, I don't want the same stuff used on her as on the other two."

"Good thinking, boss. What should I use?"

"Use her cute little scarf. That thing has been bothering me all night. Tie the knots so it looks like she tied them herself."

"Like she jumped to kill herself?"

"Yeah, that's the idea."

"Take it off, girlie," Manny said. He popped open a switchblade. "Or I take it off you myself."

Maile was more worried about the pill between her cheek and gums than a knife at her neck at that point. It was dissolving faster than what she expected. She untied the simple knot and handed it over. After an embarrassing display of affection for the scarf by Braces, her wrists were tied together with it.

"And now we leave," Lenny said. He gave Oscar a wave as he walked past him. "Goodbye, Swenberg family."

Manny stopped to say something to Oscar while leading Maile through the house. "Just remember, this was a home invasion by the Bautistas, not by us, got it?"

Oscar nodded, followed by Santos nodding.

"You know what happens when someone crosses the boss?"

Maile saw the fear in Oscar's eyes when he looked up at Manny.

"Same thing as your brothers, but twice as much fun." Manny looked at Santos. "Same goes for you, Nurse. Don't get clever."

Chapter Twelve

Maile had worn cork wedges as shoes to the Swenberg house that day, which she had already slipped off and kicked under the sideboard earlier. It wasn't much, but it might be enough as evidence that she'd been in the house that night.

Limps and Higgs led the way down the flagstone path to the boat dock, followed by Maile, with Manny right behind her, encouraging her with subtle nudges in her back with his pistol. Behind him were Lenny, and Braces brought up the rear. The gale had settled, but there was still a steady wind bringing rain from the direction of the ocean. Maile could once again smell the scent of her patchouli perfume. That was almost overpowered by the smell of the churning ocean, as she walked to the boat that would take her to…

'Stop thinking that,' she thought. 'There's a way out of this.'

That's when Maile spit her own pill toward the ground in front of her, no one else the wiser.

Limps had a hard time getting up the short ladder and over the gunwale, and Higgs wasn't much more athletic than that. It was then that Maile's plan of running and jumping into the channel was supposed to take place, but with her hands tied behind her back, and the heavy chop that continued to splash though the channel, she figured she'd drown before they could put a bullet into her. She had to go with her belief that Santos had secretly handed out sedatives instead of seasick pills. Washed down with the whisky, they should be taking effect soon.

Honey of a Hurricane

She wasn't able to manage the ladder, so hands grabbed her shoulders and lifted, while another pair of hands pushed her bottom up. Once she was over the gunwale, they weren't so gentle, and let her fall to the rain-drenched deck. The rest of the gang continued to board while she tried righting herself to a sitting position.

"Get that engine started!" Lenny called out. He went directly to the cabin below to get out of the rain.

Manny went to the controls, and after a few false starts, the engines roared to life. Braces and Higgs tossed off the lines that held the boat fast to the dock, allowing it to bounce and turn in the water even more. Maile watched as Braces went to the side and spilled his drink.

"Not much of a seasick pill!" he shouted into the wind.

"I hope some of it soaked in!" Maile called out. She didn't care if he wasn't drunk. She was hoping he got at least a little of the hypnotic sedative from the pill.

One by one, all of them retreated to the safety of the cabin, leaving only Maile sprawled on the deck, and Manny at the interior helm behind a glass window. In spite of the heavy chop in the water, he did a reasonable job of getting away from the dock and headed toward the open end of the channel. Being long and narrow, the yacht rocked from side to side as much as it did from bow to stern when going through waves. He put on only one light, something that shined directly in front of the stern, rather than illuminating the entire boat. From where she was, Maile couldn't see much, but after a few minutes, Manny gunned the engines. The boat bounced heavily several times then, salt spray came over the sides, and Maile felt they were breaking through waves that were being pushed toward shore by the wind. The boat tilted wildly at times, even turning sideways. After a few more minutes, the bouncing eased and the boat settled into forward motion.

Limps came out and went to Manny at the helm.

"Everything okay?"

"Should be smoother now," Manny shouted over the wind. "How's the boss doing?"

"Sleepin'."

"How's Braces?"

"Almost asleep." Limps wiped his face. "I might stretch out also."

"Send Higgs out here in a while. I need a rest. Been a long day."

After hearing their short conversation, Maile felt reassured that Santos had indeed switched drugs, and they were beginning to feel the effects of roofies washed down with shots of whisky. She wondered how much she'd got into her system, and hoped she'd been able to spit out most of the tablet. As it was, she felt like she could've slept then, either from the mental exhaustion of being held captive, or some mild effects from the drug.

"What about her?" Limps said, pointing his thumb at Maile.

"Later. If we toss her overboard this close to land, she'll wash ashore in an hour. Can't risk having her body get found for a couple of days, if ever."

"One of you mind helping me up into a seat?" she asked.

"Quiet, girlie," Manny said. "You're just fine where you're at."

Honey of a Hurricane

Maile watched as Limps staggered down the steps into the sleeping berth. Whatever Santos had given them was already working at putting them in drowsy states. If she could hang on and not get tossed overboard before, they might just fall asleep all at the same time.

She was able to scoot over so she was at least under an awning and mostly out of the rain. She'd never had problems with motion sickness, but the only times Maile had been on a boat was a fishing charter for a half-day trip, and on a catamaran during her honeymoon. Both had been in clear weather and calm seas. The only flights she'd ever taken were interisland flights, barely long enough to stir up trouble. But on that yacht that night, with it bouncing through heavy swells and zigzagging out to open seas, Maile was wishing she had taken a seasickness pill. All she had to keep down was part of the candy bar she'd shared with Honey, and two cans of ginger ale, but it was enough to churn in her stomach as much as the ocean was right then.

Her rising condition was back-burnered when Manny began to list to one side. When he eventually flopped onto the deck, the boat began to spin and turn in every direction seemingly at once. She still wasn't able to get to her feet because of the tossing seas, but scooted across the deck to Manny. She yelled at him through the wind and rain, trying to get him to wake up and take control at the wheel. Finding him completely out cold, Maile gave up on Manny.

She still had her hands tied behind her back. She found a way to get her feet under her by leaning against the gunwale and pushing up. By leaning her body against the wheel, she was able to keep it from free-spinning. That calmed the boat, but not her mind.

"Now what do I do?" she said, watching the floating compass built into the dashboard wobble and turn. There was another compass with a digital readout of the direction, and coordinates. They didn't mean much to her right then, if she couldn't control the wheel with her hands.

She had to let the wheel spin and the boat do whatever the storm demanded of it. She dropped to her knees, and turning sideways to him, she was able to go through Manny's pockets. There was a wallet thick with cash from the sale of Honey, and his pistol. She dropped that overboard. All that was left was a pen.

"Wait."

She knew cops often hid weapons under the cuffs of their pants. Maybe gangsters did too. She was able to scoot up one pant leg, where she found something in his sock at his ankle. Digging that out, she had a pocketknife. She got it open and began whittling at the silk scarf that bound her wrists together. It seemed like forever while the boat bounced and swayed, but she got her hands free. Hopping to her feet, she went back to the wheel and steadied the boat as best she could.

"Wait…"

She went back to get the pocketknife she'd taken off Manny and tucked it into her bra. It might come in handy later. Back at the wheel, which was spinning one way and the other by itself, she grabbed hold. Stopping the wheel didn't seem to accomplish much.

"I can't even drive a car, and I'm supposed to drive this thing in a storm?"

She still wasn't sure of the state of the men in the cabin, if they were out cold the way Manny was right then. She had to find out.

She also needed help, not just with the boat, but with the men. Seeing the radio built into the dashboard, she tried switching it on. When something lit up, she grabbed the microphone.

"What do they say on boats when there's trouble? Oh, yeah." She watched as a wave splashed over the front of the boat, sending sprays of water in every direction. "Mayday, mayday!"

She listened for a reply. Nothing came back to her. She tried a couple more knobs.

"Mayday, mayday! I'm on a boat in the ocean! I'm having trouble!"

Again, there was no response.

"Mayday, mayday?" Another wave splashed over the bow. She tossed down the microphone and took the wheel in both hands when the boat began to turn sideways. "Oh, forget it."

Unsure if boats had anything like auto-pilot, she saw nothing on the control panel labeled that way. She couldn't leave the boat to its own devices to go check on the others, even if she wasn't doing much steering as it was. She needed something to hold the steering wheel steady while she checked on the men below.

Leaning against the wheel, she pulled off her nylons and cut them in two halves with Manny's knife. Using those two pieces, she was able to tie the steering wheel to handgrips on the panel to keep it steady. Watching the compass for a moment, it settled in one direction. Then it occurred to her to cut the power a little, just to keep from going too far out to sea. Maybe the best thing was that the sky was getting light in the distance and the wind was beginning to calm ever so slightly.

"Good enough."

She went to the door of the cabin and pushed it in. She saw three forms reclined on beds, but couldn't tell who they were. With Manny on the deck, that left one man unaccounted for.

Then she heard someone in the small bathroom, losing the fight with seasickness. She figured it was Braces, the one that had been sick earlier.

She had to hurry if she wanted to get their guns from the unconscious men. Patting them down, they barely roused as she collected each of their pistols. She was just getting past the bathroom door when it opened. She rammed into it with her shoulder as she went past, slamming it closed again.

She got back up to the deck with the guns and immediately dropped them overboard. Guessing she'd been seen by Braces, she hid in a corner of the deck.

"If he finds me up here, he'll shoot me."

There was a life ring hanging on the outer wall. Pulling that free from its bracket, she stood next to the doorway that came up from the sleeping berth. Holding that out to one side, she waited.

"Hey, doll! You up there?"

The storm had settled into rain and tradewinds by then, a simple squall. She could hear his footsteps on the ladder rungs coming up.

"Come on! Let's you and me have some fun!"

She saw the toe of one foot get to the deck. Still holding the life ring, she waited until she saw his face.

Braces must've noticed the movement, because he was just turning his head as she clobbered him with the life ring square in the face. His internal lights went out faster than if she'd turned a switch, and he dropped in a heap. Tossing aside the flotation ring, she pushed him backwards into the cabin.

"Let's see you laugh about that when you wake up."

Maile rifled through drawers in the galley and cabinets in the gunwales, looking for anything she could use to tie them up. Finding a ball of twine that went with a kite, she wound several layers of string around Braces' wrists and ankles. One by one, she went around to each man, tying all of them with hands behind their backs, and ankles together. The last one to get the treatment was Manny, still out cold on the deck, his portly body listing back and forth with the movement of the boat.

"Now what do I do? I don't know which way to turn this thing to go home."

It was mostly light by then, the sun just over the horizon in the distance. She scanned the ocean but saw only water below and clouds above.

"Wait. I do know which way home is." She looked at the compass, the needle pointing near to south. "All I have to do is turn around and go north again, and that's somewhere to the left of the sunrise."

Maile untied the steering wheel and got control of the boat with her hands. She tried a gentle turn, which accomplished very little. Turning more still didn't do much. Giving the wheel a hearty spin finally made the compass move. She watched until the compass indicated north. Pushing the gas lever forward a little, she got the speed up. That also made it bounce through the swells the yacht was going through.

"Nothing like driving a car."

She tried the radio again, hitting several switches and knobs until the thing came to life. That gave her a recorded weather report. It warned all boaters to remain in shelter until the last of the storm had passed and all warnings were taken down. That was supposed to be mid-morning, according to the recorded report.

"Taken down from where?" she asked, looking out at the open ocean in front of her. She still wasn't convinced she was headed for dry land with a Hawaiian name.

Keeping her hands on the steering wheel, she turned knobs and switches on the radio, trying to figure out how to make a call.

"Okay, this thing's not a cell phone." She slapped her own forehead. "I can make a call on a cell."

Leaving the steering wheel, she rushed to search Manny's pockets for his phone, then hurried back to drive. She hit three buttons, calling for 9-1-1.

"A little ironic using a gangster's phone to call the police."

"Nine-one-one dispatch. How may I help you?" an operator asked.

"Yeah, hi. Is this Honolulu dispatch or somewhere else?"

"Honolulu. Is this an emergency call?"

"You better believe it is! I'm on a boat out at sea and I'm trying to figure out how to get back to Honolulu again. Is there someone I can talk to?"

"Ma'am, you shouldn't go out so soon. There are still storm warnings and high surf advisories in effect until noon."

"That's great, except I'm already out in the ocean and I'm trying to get back."

"Are you the captain of the vessel?" the dispatcher asked.

"What difference does it make? I'm lost!"

"The captain should know what to do."

"Unfortunately, that's me right now."

"Are you alone?" the dispatcher asked.

"Not alone but the others are out cold."

"Ma'am…"

Maile was in no mood to discuss anything. All she wanted was to get her feet on dry land. Getting away from gangsters that could wake up at any moment would be even better. "Look, I was kidnapped and taken on board this stupid boat. We drove along for maybe an hour or two. I'd really like to get back home, you know?"

"Hold on just a moment. I'll transfer your call to the Coast Guard."

It was a solid five minutes before anyone came back on the line.

"Ma'am, this is Chief Petty Officer Johnson, at Barbers Point Station. I hear you're having some trouble?"

"Sure am. Do you have a first name I can call you?"

"Samuel. What is your current status, ma'am?"

"Well, I'm on a boat out at sea. I think I'm between one and two hours south of Oahu. I don't know anything about driving boats, and everybody else is a gangster and out cold, and I'd really like to get off this boat before they wake up again."

"The good thing, ma'am, is that you're not too excited to help yourself."

"You don't know what's going on inside my head right now, Samuel."

"I suppose not, ma'am. Are you wearing a personal flotation device?"

"You mean a life vest? I guess that'd be a good idea. Just a minute." Maile rummaged through a couple of cabinets built into the hull of the boat until she found one. Turning it one way and another, she figured out how it went on. "Okay, I'm back."

"What is your current heading, ma'am?"

"I'm aimed north, according to the compass."

"Okay, good. What is your speed?"

"It says fifteen knots. Is that fast enough?"

"That's about right. What sort of craft is it?"

"A yacht, about thirty feet long. It has two engines and one mast for a sail, but the sail's not up."

"Very good. You're doing great."

"That's what you think," Maile muttered.

"What's the name of the boat? Do you know?"

"Oh boy. Wait! It's The Mongoose. It's owned by Oscar Swenberg of Hawaii Kai. That's where we left about two ago."

"Are you at the wheel right now?"

"I'm just standing here holding the wheel so the compass stays on north. Is that okay?"

"That's fine. What do you see in front of you?"

"A lot of water."

"No land? No island in the distance or anywhere on the horizon?"

"A whole lot of ocean. And Samuel? The Pacific is a very big ocean."

"Yes, ma'am, it is. I'd like you to make a course correction to north-northwest."

Maile looked at the compass with a new sense of panic. She knew enough about directions to know north was at the top, and west was to the left.

"If I split the difference, I get northwest, right? And if I split the difference again, I get north-northwest?"

"Very good. Just turn the wheel until the compass indicates the direction you want. You'll have to turn the wheel back again to keep from going in a circle."

"I already discovered that."

"Yes, ma'am?" he asked.

"Some birds are flying over me, laughing at the figure-eights I've been making in the water."

"Don't worry about the birds, ma'am. How is that course correction coming?"

"Okay, I think I have it."

"Ma'am, about the other men on the boat. You said they're out cold?"

"Um, yeah. They were drugged. I don't know how much longer they'll be asleep, though."

"You drugged them?"

"No, Santos, the nurse did." Maile used the back of her hand to wipe tears from her face that had started flowing at some point. She told herself it was rainwater. "Look, it's a long story and I'm in some trouble if these guys wake up and get loose from being tied up. Is there any way at all someone can come find me?"

"I've already dispatched a search helicopter and have a patrol boat on its way to Oahu's southern waters. You're certain you're on the leeward side, ma'am?"

"Yes. We left Hawaii Kai about two hours ago. I'm not sure, but I think we went straight out to sea from there. But I couldn't see much except for rain."

"It sound like you're still on the leeward side. That's where the helicopter is going, ma'am."

"Do they have guns? Because these guys are mean."

"How many are there, ma'am?"

"Five."

"Are they armed?"

"I took their guns and threw them overboard. I think I found them all. I didn't search them too close, though. Want me to go check for more?"

"I want you to stay at the helm. You're the skipper of that boat, until I can get someone on board to take over for you. You're doing a great job, by the way, ma'am."

"Thanks."

"It's just those five men and you and the nurse?"

"Just the men and me. The nurse is back in Hawaii Kai, where any sensible person should be."

"You should see my helicopter to the northwest soon, ma'am."

Maile looked off to one side of the boat and saw a dot in the sky. Maybe it was coming in her direction. Maybe it was a hallucination. If it wasn't someone coming to rescue her, she happily take the hallucination right then. "I think I see it. Am I supposed to do something?"

"Do you have lights on? If not, turn on as many as you can."

"Wait." Maile started hitting switches and turning knobs on the dashboard. After a moment, a few more lights came on. "Okay. Anything else I should do?"

"No. Just keep on your heading. The helicopter will fly around you at a low level to see the name of the craft. You said its name is The Mongoose?"

"Right. It's a white boat with one mast. They'll see a chubby guy tied up on the deck outside, and a woman at the steering wheel freaking out." Maile looked at Manny. He had turned onto his back and was awake, trying to get loose from his bindings. "Actually, if they could hurry, it'd be great, because these guys are starting to wake up."

"The patrol boat will be there in about half an hour. Your first contact will be with the helicopter."

"How are the people on the helicopter supposed to keep the gangsters from pitching me in the ocean if they get loose before the patrol boat gets here?" Maile laughed. "There's something I've never said before!"

"I'm glad you're maintaining a positive attitude, ma'am. The helo crew is going to drop a man on the deck of your craft to manage security."

"What? That deck's not very big and there's a mast in the way!"

The helicopter was making a circular pass around Maile and the boat right then. She gave it a hearty wave.

"The man will drop on a line from the helicopter while it maintains a hover directly over you. It will be very important for you to maintain your speed and heading as the helicopter tracks your movement."

"From how far up?"

"Thirty feet."

"The man will drop out of the helicopter while it's flying thirty feet above me, while I'm driving along?"

"Yes, ma'am."

"Wouldn't it be easier if I stopped?"

"Not really. But it's critical that you maintain your exact heading and speed that you are now. Can you tell me what that is?"

"Fifteen knots at north-northwest. That's what you told me to do."

"Just keep that heading and speed, ma'am. Don't pay any attention to the man as he comes down the line."

"Whatever." Maile looked at Manny, who was tugging at the string that held his wrists together, the same way as Maile had with her scarf earlier. She'd consider whacking him in the head, if she had something.

There was the heavy drone of a helicopter overhead, and more wind, but being inside the covered helm, she couldn't see what was happening above her. "You might want to tell him to hurry, because there's a pissed-off big guy about five feet away from me that wants nothing better than to toss me in the ocean."

Manny looked mad as a bull when he got loose from the string that was wound around his wrists. He charged for the doorway that led to where Maile was steering the boat. He was two steps away from reaching her when a man in an orange suit and helmet dropped to the deck in front of him, a cable going up into the sky. He swung an arm that clotheslined Manny, dropping him to the deck. With that, he detached from the cable and the helicopter lifted up and away. Quickly, as though it had been rehearsed, he pulled long plastic bands and secured Manny's wrists and ankles again.

"Where are the others?" the man asked Maile when he entered the tiny space she was in.

"Down below in the sleeping berth!" she shouted over the noise of the boat's engines, and that of the helicopter.

"Are they armed?"

"I'm not sure. I took pistols from their pockets, but they might have more."

"Who are they?" he asked.

"Lowlife gangsters."

He took a small, automatic assault weapon from inside his orange rescue suit and plucked a plug from the muzzle.

"What am I supposed to do?"

"Keep driving the boat."

With that, he left her with a view of Manny right in front of her, and the outline of an island in the distance. A moment later, she heard him shouting for the others to freeze. There sounded like a quick scuffle, followed by a clunk, and then silence. He was just coming back from the lower berth when the patrol boat was drawing near.

"Everything okay?" she asked.

"Okay with me. One of them's gonna need his jaw wired shut for a few weeks, though." He nudged Maile to one side and took control of the yacht. While talking in a radio microphone attached to his helmet, he eased the speed of the yacht down, allowing the patrol boat to come alongside. "Okay, someone's going come aboard to take control of this craft while I watch these guys. Do you need medical attention?"

"I'm not sure."

Maybe it was the drama, or maybe it was the sudden release of tension, but Maile dropped to the deck in a heap.

Honey of a Hurricane

Chapter Thirteen

When Maile woke up, she was on a padded bench in a small room that she didn't recognize. The bench was throbbing, moving slightly. A woman was there with her in a jumpsuit-style uniform.

"Hey, you're awake," the woman said to Maile.

Maile touched her face where it hurt. "Where am I?"

"On board a Coast Guard patrol boat. We're headed back to Barbers Point Station so you can get checked out a little better. Sorry the digs aren't a little better here, ma'am."

"What happened?"

"Near as I can tell, you were kidnapped and taken to sea, and then turned the tables on your captors. Pretty awesome stuff, ma'am."

"No, I mean how did I get on this boat?"

"I heard you passed out, and hit your head on the way down. Then a big, strong Petty Officer carried you across from the yacht to here."

"Is he okay?" Maile asked.

"He's fine. We're all worried about you."

"Who's taking care of Swenberg's yacht?"

"We've put a crew on board to bring the vessel in and manage the security of the men that kidnapped you."

Maile thought of Lenny and his gang. "Where are they?"

"Not on this vessel, so you have nothing to worry about. But how are you feeling, ma'am?"

"My head hurts." Maile was helped up to a sitting position. "Is there anything to eat?"

"We typically don't have meals on patrol boats, but I might be able to find something hot to drink."

"I don't want to take something away from one of you."

"When was the last time you ate?"

Maile touched her face again, wondering why her cheek hurt. "Yesterday morning."

When she got a cup of hot chocolate, Maile gave a quick recap of what had happened in Oscar's house the night before.

"No wonder you're hungry. How'd you know what to do? I mean, did you come up with some sort of plan of escape?"

"No pun intended, but the whole night was fluid, from beginning to end. I'm not so sure it's over yet."

"But how did you know what to do with the gangsters on the yacht?"

"Just figured it out one thing at a time, I guess. Got some help along the way."

"Help from who?"

"A nurse named Santos, and some big Coast Guard guy. Is there any way that I could thank him?"

"I can pass it along." The woman took Maile's blood pressure one last time and took off the cuff. "If you don't mind me asking, what do you do for a living?"

"Despite how I'm dressed right now, I'm actually a tour guide. I used to be a nurse, but…whatever."

"Well, if I ever get sick, I want you taking care of me." The drone of the patrol boat's engines softened, and there was a bump as though they were docking. "That should be Barbers Point. We're home and you're safe."

Maile wasn't sure why, but she started to cry. "Thanks."

The woman sat with her and put her arm around Maile's shoulders. "You're okay now. Get a meal and some sleep. Talk it out with a friend, and have a good cry. The best thing is that the bad guys are going to jail and the good guys are going home."

"Yeah, home."

When Maile was escorted beyond the dock to a waiting area inside a small building, someone was there she hoped wouldn't have met, at least for a few days. There were also several members of the press, including two camera and reporter teams from local TV stations. Somehow, they'd heard of the daring rescue at sea and needed to tell Hawaii about it. Giving back the blanket she'd been wearing, Maile bade farewell to the woman that had been watching over her.

Detective Ota pushed his way through the crowd of reporters, going straight to Maile.

"Detective Ota, imagine my shock at seeing you here."

"Are you okay? Where are your shoes?"

"I have no idea about either."

He quickly went behind her and slapped a pair of handcuffs on her wrists. He followed that by putting his coat around her.

"What's going on?" Maile asked, confused all over again.

"Just go with it. It's the only way we can get through this crowd."

"Ma'am! Ma'am! Are you the woman that was rescued?" a reporter shouted. She looked as confused as Maile was about the cuffs.

When a microphone was pushed in Maile's face and the bright light of a TV broadcast camera shone at her, Ota swept them away with his arm. "Nothing to see here."

The reporter crowded in again. "We were informed an hour ago to expect…"

"No comment!" Ota flashed his badge while making a gap between reporters and cameras. "Understand? No comment!"

"I suppose you're taking me to the station for questioning?" Maile asked once they were free from the crowd.

"I have questions, but I haven't had breakfast. Have you eaten?" he asked.

"My hosts at the Swenberg house weren't very hospitable. But there are a few things you need to know, as in ASAP. Honey has been kidnapped by a woman named Mickey. Plus, Oscar Swenberg and his nurse are tied up in his living room."

"We know all about that. Honey's safe, and Swenberg and Santos were found about an hour ago."

"Are you sure? Because Mickey just happens to be Secret Agent Hartzel from the FBI. She was the one who made the deal with Lenny, who is not a very nice man, by the way."

"Okay, it's Special Agent, not Secret Agent. And we know about the deal. Apparently, it was set up that way."

Maile stopped walking. "What?"

Ota took her by the arm to lead her forward. "I'll explain at breakfast." He removed the cuffs when they got to his car. "Sorry about that. It was the only way I could think of to get you out of there."

"Pretty handy little things, those handcuffs. You had them on me before I knew what was happening."

They stopped at a Hawaiian family restaurant, a small place Maile's mother liked going to occasionally. All the meals and most of the language served there were authentic Hawaiian, food that would've been eaten in fishing villages before European contact. Most of it was starch-heavy, and the cheaper meaty meals were for the hearty and adventurous.

Detective Ota must've known she was hungry for more than just a meal. Maile ordered a large bowl of Hawaiian stew, which was mostly leftovers turned into a thick soup, and poi. At the last minute, she told the waitress to add an order of na'au.

"Isn't na'au..." he started to ask.

"Right. Stewed intestines. Great for perking up your blood." Maile felt emotions tumbling up, and excused herself for the bathroom. She returned to the table a few minutes later. "Sorry. I needed a moment alone."

"At least. Everything okay now?" he asked.

"Mostly. What's the deal with Hartzel, or Mickey, whatever her name really is?"

"That's partly my fault," Ota said. "When we met that day to discuss her plan, she said she wasn't running her operation any time soon, and I took that to mean in the next few weeks. In her world, soon apparently means in the next few hours."

"And I ended walking into the middle of her operation?" she asked.

"That's the way it looks."

"You know what that…what she did to me?" Maile asked.

"I might've heard something. Tell me in your words."

"That…" Maile bit her tongue. "She left me there with those guys, with Lenny and his crew. She could've bought me to get me out of there, but backed out. What's that all about?"

"I think it has less to do with you personally than it does with a fed thinking local cops interfered with her operation."

"I'm not a cop! How did I interfere?" Maile waited until the waitress delivered their meals. "She left me there with gangsters, Detective. She knew they were going to kill me later."

"Do you have evidence of that? Because I can bring charges of…"

Maile shook her hands in the air out of frustration. "Forget the evidence. Just once, forget about the stupid evidence! She was going to allow them to drop me in the ocean miles out to sea during a storm, with my hands tied behind my back. She knew that."

"Maile, the feds play by a different set of rules than we do, than I do. I'm sorry. I never suspected she was going there this weekend. If I had known, I never would've let you go near the place."

"Why didn't you come looking for me? I was hours past when you were supposed to pick me up."

"I did. I drove past several times. I even parked and started for the door when the rain was starting. One of the neighbors was just coming back down the walkway. He denied seeing anyone that looked like you in the house.

"That must've been the Boy Scout."

"Who?" he asked.

"The neighborhood block watch captain came by once after the electricity went out to check on us. I'm surprised he's not in a shallow grave in the Swenberg backyard. When he said I wasn't there, what did you do?" she asked.

"I left. When I got back to town, I checked at your apartment, the Manoa Tours office, and even with your brother at your mother's house. Nobody knew where you were, including Lopaka."

"Nobody should've known." Maile took another deep breath to settle her nerves again. "I still feel like letting someone have it." Maile got started on the na'au. "What about Honey? Where did Hartzel drop her off? In some homeless camp, I suppose?"

"Honey is in the hospital. Somehow, she'd gotten her hands on several sedatives and washed them down with booze right before they left the house."

"Oh." Maile figured it was the roofies. "She's okay?"

"She should be, after a stint in detox."

"What about Oscar and Santos? They're okay?"

"Oscar's also in the hospital. A little dehydrated and getting some treatment for his fractures, but he should be going home in a couple of days."

"Santos wasn't the best nurse I've ever come across, but she saved my life last night."

"What'd she do?"

"She knew Lenny and his boys were going to pitch me overboard once we were out to sea. She laid out pills on the bar, along with shots of whisky, telling them they were seasick pills. They were actually roofies that Manny had been giving Honey to perk up her performance in the bedroom. I guess the other girls that were there earlier in the week got them also, including Suzie."

"They were forced or took them on their own volition?" Ota asked.

"I got the idea they didn't have much choice."

"What about you?"

"Lenny and the boys were surprised when I showed up. They were done with, well, having women drop in. They had other things on their minds with Mickey coming for their big business deal. I was simply in the way."

"How did Santos help you?" he asked.

"The roofies got them sedated enough that I was able to deal with them one at a time on the boat by tying them up. The shot of whisky accelerated the effect, I guess so they'd fall asleep faster, before they could throw me overboard. Great plan. I almost didn't notice it until too late."

"You didn't take one?" he asked.

"I cheeked it the way psych patients do, then spit it out later." She told him about Braces, the only one that didn't go completely out, and how she had to clobber him with the life ring. "That was after I threw their guns overboard. Glad I didn't keep one, because I'm not sure if I wouldn't have used it on one or two of them."

"You didn't, and that's what matters. But just so you know, you didn't find all of them."

"That must've been the loud clunk I heard when the Coast Guardsman went into the lower berth where I had them tied up."

"I still need to talk to them."

She pushed her empty bowl of na'au away. "Okay, now for the very large elephant in a very small room. I thought Lenny was an informant that worked with you guys?"

"I thought so, too. He sure had the wool pulled over our eyes."

"He played all of you?" Maile asked, beginning on her bowl of poi.

"That's something for Internal Affairs to investigate. There might be a shakeup in the detective squad once they're done."

"I don't know what that means, and I don't care. Lenny made a lot of noise about finding some safe deposit keys that are supposed to be in the Swenberg Box. Any idea of what those are supposed to be for?"

"We need to get him and his boys in interrogation rooms to find out a lot of things." He pushed away his empty plate. "Sure would be nice to have that box, though."

"Lenny seemed to think the keys were in the box, and that they were for a safe deposit box. I still can't figure out why Frank was taking the box into the ocean that day at Hanauma Bay. Nobody's had any explanation for that at all."

"Your friend, Santos, knows something about that."

"Why her? Why would Oscar divulge something to his nurse that might be incriminating?"

"She's anything but a nurse. She's also a fed, Secret Service out of the San Francisco office."

"She was working with Hartzel, Mickey, whatever her name is this week?"

"Separate operations, according to Santos. Since they work for different agencies, they'd never met, even though they both worked in the same state, only four hundred miles apart."

"Maybe I hit my head on the boat a little too hard, but I don't get it."

"Santos was running an operation investigating Hartzel's activities. Large amounts of counterfeit money has been flooding California, and has been traced back to Honolulu. That money that Hartzel paid for Honey was probably counterfeit."

"And Santos was pretending to be a private duty nurse in Swenberg's house, hoping to witness something about Hartzel passing bad money?"

"They might've been thinking Oscar Swenberg had something to do with the counterfeiting operation. Or maybe his brothers. Who knows? She didn't elaborate," Ota said. "But she was watching out for you last night, with the pill thing. I doubt someone else would've thought of that scheme."

"Oh, I'm not so sure. I know some people that would've thought of it."

"Who?"

"Nurses. I'm the one that recognized the scheme, and spit the pill out later, after all."

He raised his glass of water to her in a salute. "To nurses."

"Got that right." She tapped her glass against his. "There's something else. I might have some evidence for you about Frank's murder."

"When I talked to Oscar yesterday, he continued to deny knowing anything about it."

"I think it was Lenny, or at least his gang behind Frank's murder."

"Why? Did one of them say something about it?" Ota asked.

"No, but I did get a knife from one of them, the one named Manny."

"Where is it?"

"It's, well…" Maile reached into her halter-top for the pocketknife that had been hidden there for the last several hours. "Maybe the blade on that will match the wound in Frank's eyeball. And check the Swenberg's kitchen for a set of metal-handled knives. One of the set is missing, a filet knife according to Honey. And it was the bartender named Higgs that was fond of using one from that set of knives to slice lemons."

She handed over Manny's pocketknife with a shudder. Ota took it and placed it in an evidence bag that he always seemed to have in a pocket. "Are you sure you don't want to work for the police department?"

***

On Sunday morning, there was a knock at Maile's door.

She didn't bother lifting her head to reply. "Not today, Rosamie."

There was another more insistent knock.

"No tea today, Rosamie. Go to church."

After more knocking, Maile wrapped in her sheet and peeked out the peephole. She unlocked all the locks except for the security chain. "Detective Ota, what brings you here way too early on a Sunday morning?"

"Apparently, not tea. Have a tour to give this morning, Ms. Spencer?"

"I have several hours more sleep to get and a headache to deal with. Why?"

"Can you come to the station downtown after you're fed and dressed? You might want to do something about that shiner, too."

Maile touched her tender cheek and eye. "You know I don't like coming to the police station."

"I have your stuff, including your shoes that you left behind at Swenberg's place the other night."

She opened the door a little more. "You have my phone?"

"And a few other things. You need to come claim them."

"Are there messages on the phone?"

"I'm not your personal secretary, Ms. Spencer."

"You're calling me by my last name because you need to speak to me in some official capacity?"

"Very good."

"Should I dress to fight with Suzie in a cell, or will I be coming home later?"

"No cell today, but there is something important to discuss. Quite a few things, in fact."

Maile wrapped a little tighter and pushed hair from her face. There was a good reason for her to go in that day: to get the money she was owed for the night of work at the Swenberg house. "Give me a couple of hours to become human and I'll be there."

***

Maile needed to run a couple of errands on her way to the police station downtown. One was to a local coffee shop for an extra-large cup of energy. The other was to the Manoa House to get the Swenberg Box that she had hidden there.

Without her personal key ring, she used the key that was hidden in the garden to let herself into the Manoa House. She had to dig through a desk drawer to find the key that went to the locked drawer where Swenberg's box was hidden. She was a little nervous sliding open the drawer, that in some weird magical way, it had disappeared in the days since she put it there. When she found it as she left it, Maile was a little disappointed, that the mystery of the box, and its contents was nearly over. It had brought so much trouble into her life, and grief into others', that it really was time to hand it over to its next victim. That's almost what the thing had become, a talisman of bad luck to whoever had it at any given time.

Taking it out of the drawer and tucking it at the bottom of her bag, she left for the police station.

She knew better than to sit near the middle exit door on the bus, that strange things happened when seated there with the box on her lap. Instead, she stayed near the front of the bus, watching out the front window for any dangers that might be lurking ahead. What she could do if something came at her in a rush she wasn't sure, but at least she'd know before it happened.

Maile saw her stop coming and went to the exit door with several others. The main police station was in the middle of Honolulu's modest downtown, surrounded by parks and older buildings. Not far away was the Iolani Palace, where she often took tours.

When a few tourists went off in search of an afternoon of entertainment, Maile and a pair of young women went to the police station. She listened to them gripe about someone that needed bailing out of trouble once again. It sounded like one was the jailbait's wife, while the other was his sister, and neither of them were too happy about turning over their hard-earned money as bail for a guy that was getting slapped with all kinds of four letter words.

Even though she wanted to see what the guy looked like, she was glad to leave the angry pair behind when she went into the lobby. A cheerful young woman clerk in a simple police uniform was tending the information desk.

"Detective Ota is expecting me."

The clerk peeled a sticky note from her desk and looked up. "You're Maile? I mean, Ms. Spencer?"

"Yes, that's right. Is he in?"

"We've...he's been waiting for you." The clerk seemed to beam approval at Maile's presence. "Please, come with me."

As she was led through a maze of corridors to the squad room where Detective Ota had his desk, officers watched Maile go by.

"Hey, what's going on?" she asked the clerk. "Why's everybody staring at us?"

"Not us, you. You're like a celebrity around here today."

"Me? Why?"

Maile never got her answer, but was let into the squad room. Officer Brock Turner was there, almost as if he were waiting.

"There she is! Good looking shiner, Maile."

"Hi Br...Officer Turner." Maile helplessly smiled at him. She felt that if she were a dog, her tail would be wagging back and forth. Unfortunately, the makeup she'd used wasn't hiding her prize leftover from the night on the yacht. "Yeah, another shiner."

"I hear you had an exciting night over the weekend?"

"Oh, yes, the storm. Funny how easy it is to forget about a storm as quickly as it passes."

His face turned more serious. "Is your mother's cottage okay?"

"She's fine. Kenny was there with her. They got through it okay. A little wet, but okay."

"Maybe I'll swing by later and check on them. I think Detective Ota is waiting for you."

Ota was at his desk, a place Maile had come to get to know quite well. But it was being watched and smiled at by the others in the room that bothered Maile so much. He had a thick stack of paperwork on his desk that he seemed to be going through and signing, one sheet at a time.

"Detective Ota, what's going on?"

"Just another day in paperwork paradise. Why?"

"Why is everyone looking at me?"

"Oh, them. They just want to see the person who brought down one of Hawaii's biggest crime syndicates single-handedly, and was responsible for the capture of two bank robbers, all in one day."

"That's me?"

"When Lenny Gallo and his little gang and jailhouse jerks was finally locked in cells all at the same time, it was cause for celebration."

"The Coast Guard and you guys did that, not me. What's this about two bank robbers?" she asked. Whenever the least bit of confusion crept in, she tapped her puffy cheek.

"The Bautista brothers. You don't remember?"

"Remember what?"

"There was a bank robbery on the day you went to the Swenberg house. The culprits, the Bautista brothers, stole the fishing boat Lenny had chartered for his get-away."

"What did I have to do with that?" she asked.

"When you were on the Coast Guard patrol boat headed back to Oahu, you told them about the Bautistas in the fishing boat. They were able to send out another search crew and found them floundering in the channel halfway to Maui. Not only did you save their lives, you provided the information that led to their capture. There's even reward money coming your way."

"Reward?" That perked up Maile's attitude. "When do I get that?"

"Probably not for several weeks. But that's why you're being celebrated."

"Don't try and turn me into some sort of hero. While you think I captured those guys, I was trying to find a way of getting away from them. That's all."

A few of the other officers and detectives gathered around Ota's desk to hear Maile's short version of Lenny's capture.

"As far as we're concerned, you took the biggest risks. You also provided enough evidence against them to put them in prison for the rest of their lives." Ota looked at her bag. "You bring it?"

"Yeah. You have my envelope?"

He opened his desk drawer for two plain white envelopes that he put on his desk.

Maile got the box out of her bag and held it on her lap.

"Did you open it?" he asked.

"No. Why are there two envelopes?"

He pushed one envelope to the side of the desk nearest her. "This one has the agreed amount in it."

"What's the other one for?"

He pushed it forward. "This one has twice as much in it."

"Why twice as much?"

Ota glanced up at the other cops around them. "It's counterfeit, taken from the money Lenny got the other night from Agent Hartzel. The rest of it is evidence, but no one will ever notice a few bills missing from it."

"I don't want counterfeit money."

"You may as well take it. The stuff's so good, even the bank wouldn't notice it was fake when you deposited it."

"We agreed on a certain amount of money for me to do that job the other night. Which envelope is that?" she asked.

He tapped his finger on one. "This."

"It's real American money?"

"Absolutely authentic in every way."

She snatched the envelope and tucked it into a pocket. Then she put the box on his desk.

Ota put away the other envelope before looking up at the other cops around them. "See what I mean? Honolulu's most honest citizen."

Maile got an 'attagirl' and felt a squeeze to a shoulder as the others drifted away.

"That was a test, to see if I'm honest?"

Ota picked up the box for a close examination. "No. I knew you'd take the right amount. I just wanted to show the others that there are still decent people in the world."

"I didn't feel so decent at the Swenberg house the other night."

"Lenny had a way of making people feel badly about themselves."

"You gonna open that thing or what?" she asked.

"You think I should?"

"Personally, I think it should be tossed in a bonfire at the beach. But you want evidence, so yeah, open it."

He gave it a shake and something rattled inside. "You told me there're keys to safe deposit boxes inside, and Santos from the Secret Service confirmed that."

"According to Lenny, anyway. Safe deposit boxes on the mainland. Did Santos say which banks?" she asked.

Honey of a Hurricane

"Didn't say one way or another. But she's already headed back to the mainland, and left the keys with me."

"Why didn't she take them with her?" Maile asked.

"Maybe I neglected to mention you were bringing the box in today."

"Does Oscar know anything about them?"

"I have news about him I'll tell you in a minute. When I asked him about the box at the hospital yesterday, he said he had no idea what was inside, and wanted nothing to do with the box. I tend to believe him."

"If he doesn't care and Santos didn't want the keys any more than that, I say throw the box in the dumpster where it belongs. Opening it will only lead to more trouble."

"Maybe so, but I'm a police officer, and trouble is my career."

Ota got a wire pick from his desk drawer and made quick work of the lock. If the lock was simple, the seal that went around the edges was solid. A set of keys dropped out when he pried the box open. There were four keys all together, each of them looking like they fit cabinet drawers rather than doors.

"Are those safe deposit box keys?" Maile asked.

"You've never seen one?"

"Never had anything valuable enough to need safe keeping."

"Huh," he said. "I would've thought you'd say something about your soul being your most prized possession."

"That I trust to the gods."

He kept looking at the keys one by one. "Which gods?"

"Any that're paying attention to me at any given moment. Lately, I've needed a whole team of them."

"Never been a religious man." He looked at each key closely. None of them were marked with bank names, only box numbers. They were all different styles as though they belonged to different banks. "Looks like I'm going to spend the rest of the day figuring out which bank vaults these go to."

Maile picked up the empty box for a closer look. There was still something else inside, a photograph that was enclosed in a ziplocked bag. She took it out.

"You'll have some fun with this, too."

He looked at the picture. "Who are they?"

Maile took the picture back again. There was a man and woman standing next to each other as though they were on vacation. Behind them was a detail from an architectural old building built in a Spanish style, weather and time stained. The sky was blue overhead, their shadows were at their feet, and the sidewalk they were on was paved with concrete tiles.

"That's our Santos, but I don't know the guy. Another Swenberg, maybe?"

Ota took the picture back. "That's Santos? I never got too good of a look at her."

"Definitely her, maybe a few years ago and a different hairstyle."

"How can you be so sure?"

"Look at the end of her left eyebrow in the picture. There's a mole, right?"

"So?"

"Now she has a scar in the exact same spot. Barely noticeable, but her eyebrow isn't quite perfect there. She probably weighs five or ten pounds more now than she did in the picture, but that's definitely her."

"Is there anything you don't see?" he asked, now looking at the picture with a magnifying glass.

"Nurse, remember? I'm supposed to notice things about people. Anyway, women have a way of checking out the competition. It makes us happy when we can find a flaw in someone."

She watched as he bagged the ziplocked baggie as evidence and sent it for fingerprint analysis.

"You had something to tell me about Oscar Swenberg?"

"Have you been to see him in the hospital?" he asked.

"I'm done visiting Swenbergs in hospitals, or anywhere else."

"You didn't visit him or his nurse last night?"

"No, why?"

"Where were you last night?" he asked.

"At home, in bed, sound asleep. You woke me this morning, remember? Why? What's going on with him? Is he okay?"

"That's what the rest of us would like to know. Somehow, he disappeared from his hospital bed last night."

Maile could only laugh. She stood, collected her bag, and straightened her chair. "Have a nice time with your next mystery, Detective Ota."

"Where will you be if I need to find you?"

"Giving a peaceful and respectful tour of the Iolani Palace." Maile looked across the squad room where someone was headed for the door. "What's she doing here?"

"Who?" Ota looked at where Maile was glaring. "Special Agent Hartzel? She had paperwork to finish on her case. I hope she's leaving once and for all."

Maile dropped her bag to the floor and went after Hartzel, tracking her down in the middle of the busy room. Ota called after her, but she didn't listen.

"I want a word with you."

Hartzel stopped, but didn't bother smiling. "Make it quick. I have a plane to catch."

"Have a nice flight home." Maile raised her hand and swung. Her palm caught Hartzel's cheek with full force. "Take that with you as a souvenir from someone you met in Hawaii."

Maile strode away. Passing by Ota's desk, she grabbed her bag.

"You got a problem with that?" she asked him.

"Not at all.

...

Honey of a Hurricane

More from Kay Hadashi

<u>Maile Spencer Honolulu Tour Guide Mysteries</u>
AWOL at Ala Moana
Baffled at the Beach
Coffee in the Canal
Dead on Diamond Head
Honey of a Hurricane
Keepers of the Kingdom
Malice in the Palace
Peril at the Potluck

<u>Gina Santoro Mysteries</u>
Unknown Victim
Hidden Agenda
And more!

<u>The June Kato Intrigue Series</u>
Kimono Suicide
Stalking Silk
Yakuza Lover
Deadly Contact
Orchids and Ice
Broken Protocol

<u>The Island Breeze Series</u>
Island Breeze
Honolulu Hostage
Maui Time
Big Island Business
Adrift
Molokai Madness
Ghost of a Chance

The Melanie Kato Adventure Series
Away
Faith
Risk
Quest
Mission
Secrets
Future
Kahuna
Directive
Nano

The Maui Mystery Series
A Wave of Murder
A Hole in One Murder
A Moonlit Murder
A Spa Full of Murder
A Down to Earth Murder
A Haunted Murder
A Plan for Murder
A Misfortunate Murder
A Quest for Murder
A Game of Murder

The Honolulu Thriller Series
Interisland Flight
Kama'aina Revenge
Tropical Revenge
Waikiki Threat
Rainforest Rescue

Honey of a Hurricane

Made in the USA
Columbia, SC
10 January 2025